BRIEF
LIVES

BRIEF LIVES

Suzanne Foster
and Pamela Smith

Foreword by
Anton Obholzer BSc MB ChB DPM FRCPsych
Chairman, The Tavistock Clinic, London

Introduction by
Colin Murray Parkes MD FRCPsych
Senior Lecturer, Academic Department of Psychiatry
Consultant Psychiatrist, The London Hospital

Arlington Books
King Street, St. James's
London S.W.1
in association with Thames Television

BRIEF LIVES
First Published in England 1987 by
Arlington Books (Publishers) Ltd
15–17 King Street, St. James's
London SW1

© *Suzanne Foster & Pamela Smith,*
Thames Television PLC 1987

Typeset by Rapidset, London
Printed and bound by
Biddles Ltd, Guildford

British Library Cataloguing in Publication Data

Foster, Suzanne
Brief lives
1. Bereavement—Psychological aspects
2. Parent and child
I. Title II. Smith, Pamela
306.8'8 BF575.G7

ISBN   0–85140–706–4

The Authors

The authors, Suzanne Foster and Pamela Smith, were joint researchers for the Thames Television series *Brief Lives*. In the course of making the programmes, they spoke to over 200 bereaved parents as well as professionals in medicine, in the media and the police. Through their accounts we hear at first hand of the feelings that arise when a child dies.

Contents

Foreword, 9

Introduction, 11

1   **How *Brief Lives* Began,** 15

2   **Accidents Do Happen,** 17
Families whose children have died as the result of an accident talk about how they are coping with their loss

3   **The Thread of Uncertainty,** 27
The team of professionals who work on the Cancer Ward at Great Ormond Street Hospital discuss their work

4   **Childhood Cancer: Cheryl,** 33
Cheryl's parents decided to look after their daughter at home as she was dying of cancer

5   **Life Sentence,** 41
The problems faced by the families of murdered children

6   **Suicide,** 49
Two families talk about losing their children through suicide

7   **Anorexia Nervosa: Catherine,** 57
Catherine died after seven years of fighting the disease

Dos and Don'ts for Well Meaning Friends and Relatives, 67

The Compassionate Friends, 71

Appendix One
Further Reading
   Books, 74
   Articles, 77

Appendix Two
Counselling and Bereavement Organisations
   General, 78
   Specific, 81

Appendix Three
Dinah's Diary, 90

Foreword

The trend in recent years for the production of well-researched and sensitively produced television programmes in the field of human relations is to be warmly welcomed. The books that often accompany the series serve a doubly useful purpose—on the one hand, to consolidate the understanding arising from the programmes, on the other, to make a clear, independent contribution to a field so often spoilt by professional jargon.

Brief Lives addresses itself to the death of a child in the family. As both book and programmes show, it is a mistake to believe that people 'naturally' take to the mourning process. Defences against the pain of the loss abound; in the parents, the family, the neighbourhood, and in society and its institutions. The end result of this defensive process is that the death often remains as a hindering presence interfering with the quality of life of all those left behind. The mourning process is not only about grieving the deceased, it is also about enabling mourners to free themselves for other relationships. Siblings of the deceased often have to bear a heavy load of both personal and parental pain, and nothing is as tragic as a child conceived and treated as a replacement for a dead one rather than being a child in its own right.

This book addresses the subject of loss and bereavement in a clear and methodical way; its examples help to identify the problems and, most importantly, to give information and courage for people to intervene in their own personal situations. In so doing, it helps to minimise the impact of the inevitable disturbance and to maximise the personal growth and maturity that is inherent in the loss.

Dr Anton Obholzer
Chairman, The Tavistock Clinic, London

Introduction

'I am very hungry, mother!' His mother said to him 'Tomorrow, dear Willie, we'll have some bread.'. . . Presently he was silent, and his mother saw a smile upon his lips. . . . She knew that he was dying. He just said to her, 'Tomorrow, tomorrow, mother', and he died.
Just then the cathedral clock struck twelve—the mother counted it. God had given him that day his 'daily bread' . . . he had found his place of refuge.

Rev. James Vaughan MA
Sermons to Children
Christchurch, Brighton (1888)

To people brought up in the second half of the 20th century children's stories about death in childhood seem morbid and frightening. Surely we should protect our children from such worrying thoughts; besides, what can we tell them when we ourselves are at a loss?

Victorian children's stories reflect an age when people had large families because they expected many of their children to die. Death in childhood was common, it took place at home more often than in hospital and tradition demanded that family and friends gathered at the bedside to ensure the child's safe passage to a better world. Religious faith provided a meaning for death and a set of rituals to accompany it. Grief was a normal, expected reaction which was openly experienced and shared.

Today the situation is very different. Science has pushed death into old age (or we like to pretend it has) and most people die tidily behind drawn screens in a hospital. Cremation services take place at 30-minute intervals during which an unknown clergyman recites words that are unfamiliar to a congregation who no longer congregate each Sunday or see themselves as part of a caring community. Nobody cries, or if they do they apologise for letting the side down. Grief has become a guilty secret; mourning a private affair. Death itself is a hateful tearing apart of the comfortable assumptions on which our security is based. And those who cannot contain their distress are advised to seek help from doctors as if grief were itself some kind of illness.

When a child dies, the family can no longer avoid this stark reality. Others may also choose to face these problems out of sympathy for a friend in need, or simply because they find it wiser to look at the dark side of life rather than to ignore its existence. Just as tragedy is often more rewarding than comedy so the anticipation of death and grief may leave us better able to cope with these things when, at length, they come our way.

Despite all the advances of modern science 10 in every 1000 children born will die before the age of 1, and another 6 will be stillborn. The commonest causes of death in infancy are congenital abnormalities and complications of birth. Among those who survive the first week of life the commonest cause of death during the next 3 months is the so-called 'Sudden Infant Death Syndrome', a bewildering condition for which doctors can give no adequate account. Thereafter accidents are the most common.

Road traffic accidents account for half the accidental deaths but fatal accidents at home are also all too common. Among the illnesses which cause the death of children many are the consequence of inborn abnormalities which arise in the womb and cannot be corrected.

These account for many stillbirths and neonatal (within the first week of life) deaths. In later childhood, cancer of the brain and blood account for many deaths and whereas some blood cancers can now be successfully treated there are others for which no remedy is possible.

Murder and manslaughter are still uncommon causes of death

in childhood, as is suicide, although there has been a worrying increase in deaths by suicide among adolescents in recent years. These deaths have consequences for families which point to a need for special care and concern.

Thames Television faced a daunting task with the inception of a series of programmes on death in childhood. They have allowed families who have suffered awful loss to express their sorrow and their rage while offering no easy answers. But this does not mean that answers are lacking. The answers which do emerge, slowly and painfully, are convincing because they come from the sufferers, the bereaved and those experts (doctors, nurses, social workers, and others) whose responsibility is to care for the dying and the bereaved. These are no armchair philosophers but men and women who have learned the hard way, by experiencing or sharing, and they are not easily satisfied by simplistic solutions be they in the form of drugs or prayers or old wives' tales. Not that drugs or prayers or folk wisdom are without value, but they need to be seen as part of a range of possibilities and to be offered out of an understanding of the special needs of particular people rather than out of a blanket assumption that 'all you need is a tranquilliser, a verse from the Bible, or to keep busy'.

For there is hope: despite the worst that fate or man can bring, with help from the rest of us, people can come through and may even grow in emotional stature in the face of death.

Dr Colin Murray Parkes
Senior Lecturer in Psychiatry
London Hospital Medical College

1

How *Brief Lives* Began

The idea for making the series *Brief Lives* came from Julian Aston, one of the series' producer/directors, whose own son Luke died in an accidental fire in May 1985, just before his eighth birthday. After Luke's death Julian could find no purpose for living. His whole world had been turned upside down. He felt guilty, full of anger and self pity.

After several months when he felt like giving up, Julian contacted *Compassionate Friends*, a self-help group for parents whose children have died. Through these meetings, he realised that he was not alone in his experience, that other parents were living with the loss of their children, and that others had suffered even worse tragedies than his own. He came to the conclusion that a TV series on this subject might be helpful.

Julian took the idea to Alan Horrox, the Controller of Education at *Thames Television*, who commissioned the series and assembled a team including producer–directors Polly Bide, Jill Fullerton Smith and Michael Whyte, and researchers Suzanne Foster and Pamela Smith, with Gillian McCredie as co-producer. They decided that the series would focus on accidental death, childhood cancer, murder, suicide and anorexia.

Whilst researching the series the team talked to over 200 bereaved parents. Some had lost a child very recently and others many years previously. Their grieving did not necessarily follow any set pattern and the way parents were coping with the death of their child varied enormously from one individual to another. Perhaps the most important factor in learning to cope with a child's death was the amount of support received from family and friends.

The overwhelming need of all the parents who contacted us was to talk about the death of their child. Many people spoke of there being no-one to talk to; that friends and acquaintances would avoid or ignore them. Often family and friends expected the grief to diminish or disappear after a few months, 'Oh you must be feeling better by *now*', was a common complaint.

The strain on marriages after bereavement is immense. Husbands and wives grieve differently. Husbands are often able to absorb themselves in their work, whereas wives, especially those at home, have more time to dwell on their grief. Among those who contacted the team, many said that the bereavement had caused tremendous resentment between partners, and some marriages had ended in divorce. Sisters and brothers, too, were deeply affected and their feelings were sometimes overlooked by parents who were absorbed in their own sorrow.

Some parents directed their feelings of anger at the professionals who they felt had handled the bereavement poorly. General practitioners were accused of being too eager to prescribe tranquillisers rather than take time to talk about the death or recommend counselling. The police, too, were sometimes accused of tactlessness in delivering bad news.

Although it is clear that parents never 'get over' the death of their child, for many it is possible given time, and with love and support, to come to terms with the loss. It is a slow and painful journey, as we heard from the parents in *Brief Lives*.

2

Accidents Do Happen

After stillbirth and neonatal death, accidents are the most common cause of death in children. In 1985, 1200 children died in accidents in Great Britain.

The first film of the television series focused on the experiences of four families who lost a child through accidental death, and was introduced by Julian Aston who lost his own son, Luke, in a fire 2 years ago. We see how, through the feelings of initial shock, disbelief and anger, these families have come to a gradual sense of resolution over their child's death and to a realisation that life is worth living after the death of a child.

Dinah's son Jamie was 14 years old when, in 1985, his motorcycle went out of control and crashed through a plate glass window.

Pat and Roger's son Craig was 12 years old when, in 1983, he was killed by a lorry whilst out cycling.

In 1979, Edna and John's daughter Mandy was hit by a car on her way back from Sunday School. She was 9 years old.

Vic and Hazel lost their son Philip in 1986, when he was 17 years old. He was hit by a motorcyclist.

For each of the families the news of their child's death was traumatic. Unlike death after, for example, a period of illness, parents have no time to prepare for the loss. Dinah expresses the intensity of her emotions at the time:

'I felt at first as if my whole insides had been scraped out and I

was empty, but bleeding, really, really raw as though something had connected me and Jamie and now it was completely severed and it was raw from that.'
Roger's feelings were similar:
'I thought there was no way we would get over the dreadful pain and awful hurt inside, which you can't explain to people. And it was total darkness even in the middle of the day when there was bright sunshine. In my mind it was just total darkness.'

Pat had found the first 12 months unbearable, but thought things might begin to improve after a year; they did not:
'I found myself completely at sea. I didn't feel I could go on coping any longer. I felt I had coped for 12 months and there was no more energy left. The mental stress was making me physically tired and I could no longer cope with it.'

Edna did not feel comforted by the fact that she had two other children:
'People said to me "Well you've got two other children, you're lucky," but that didn't seem to matter. Mandy had gone and nothing made sense any more. I just couldn't cope.'

As time passed after the deaths of their children, the parents continued to have difficulty coping. Most found that friends and acquaintances avoided talking about the dead child. This was most hurtful because it was as if the child had never existed. Sometimes friends would even avoid meeting them altogether. Edna:
'So many people just crossed over to the other side of the road. When I did finally go out, then I'd see somebody and think, oh, here's a chance to talk, and they'd just ignore me. That did hurt very much.'

It may be difficult to know how to help a bereaved person. They are often isolated in their own grief and unwittingly reject other people's attention. Stephen, Edna's son, remembers being virtually left to fend for himself while his parents were grieving. Talking about his mother he says:
'She'd completely gone into herself really. She used to sit there crying all day, you know, a lot, for weeks, well, months, practically.'

Edna and John were unable to share their grief, and used to cry alone. Things became so bad between them that they seriously considered divorce and even went as far as putting their house up for sale. It was only the intervention of their two sons that made them reconsider.

Roger and Pat also grieved differently from one another, causing problems in their marriage. They found themselves arguing constantly and Pat felt resentful towards Roger for being able to go out to work while she remained at home caring for their 2 year old daughter:

'There were times when she wanted to play or do a jigsaw and all I wanted to do was climb into my bed. I just wanted time to grieve. That's why I felt angry with Roger because I used to feel he's got his lunch hour to grieve.'

Their anger and guilt was affecting their relationship with their other children and, like Edna and John, their marriage came close to ending. Roger considered himself a failure because of Craig's death. He felt that he may in some way have been able to prevent it; he had passed the accident minutes after it happened and felt that if he had stopped, things might have been different.

All the parents went through feelings of anger—towards the person who caused the accident, towards themselves, even towards the dead child. It took Dinah 6 months to let her anger out, but when she finally did begin to release it she felt:

'angry at the whole fact that you come into life, you love people, they die. In the past, lots of painful things had happened to me before, but nothing to equal that. . . I didn't know that I could be hurt so completely and so totally. So I felt fury, outrage.'

After some time, for all the families, a form of resolution emerged. Roger and Pat realised that in order to save their marriage communication was essential, and so they talked to each other endlessly about their feelings, and they learned to respect their differences.

All the parents quoted here are members of *Compassionate Friends*. For them, talking to others with a similar loss helped them come to terms with their grief. It is difficult for people outside the experience to understand the intensity of their feelings

but even the smallest gesture can help, as Edna recalls:
'Just to touch a person, that means an awful lot, because somebody did do that to me. Somebody came up and just touched my
arm and walked away and I've never forgotten that.'

Gradually with support and kindness and, most of all, time,
parents do feel life is worth carrying on. As Roger says:
'I have come to terms with it now. The hurt is still there, tremendous sadness. There's an emptiness within me, which I feel will
possibly always be there. But I can cope now and I feel that because we're back together, as a family (that's probably been the
biggest difference to me, that's helped me to come to terms with
it), I feel that there *is* life after losing someone, because no-one
can erase that person from your mind.'

A Son is Killed

Martin Colebrook GP
a professional who has lost a child

Our wedding anniversary was on a warm and sunny Sunday in
August. The family was gathering for lunch although Nic, our
medical student son, had not yet returned from a run on his
motorcycle after lavishing tender loving care on his pride and joy
the previous day. The meal was early so we had hardly noticed
his absence. Then we saw a policeman walking up the drive,
'Who has been misbehaving now?' was the jocular reaction
among us.

I welcomed him in the usual affable manner, but there was no
smile in return. He said that a motor-cyclist had had an accident a
few miles away and papers found on the machine showed that it
was Nic's. We knew Nic kept his documents in his pocket so it
had to be he who was, as the constable said, 'critical' in the local
hospital.

I left the family attempting to eat lunch and drove to the accident and emergency department. A junior nurse was detailed to

talk to me, the anxious relative, while I waited. Poor girl, she did not know what to say, but I was able to chat her along as my mind went into a verbose and almost schizoid detachment from the main issue.

Soon the orthopaedic consultant came to speak to me. His manner rendered the details of his news superfluous. 'Fixed dilated pupils, severe brain damage, on a ventilator. I have to say that the outlook for survival is not good. Police escort to Queen's Square has been arranged. Would you like to see him?' All said with the utmost sympathy, but the message was clear. I entered the resuscitation room.

It was Nic all right, but far from being all right. All the technical hardware had been attached and the ambulance was waiting.

My wife and I drove to London and located the National Hospital for Nervous Diseases in a frustrating maze of one-way streets. We sat in the ward waiting room. The houseman came and said the outlook was poor, then the senior registrar, equally pessimistic but more authoritatively so. He offered to bring the consultant, but I saw no point. The case was straightforward; straightforwardly bad.

We said we had agreed with Nic when he first went motorcycling that his kidneys and any other useful organs should be made available if he died. Then we entered the ward and sat beside him.

There was even more apparatus than before, yet he simply looked asleep; his skin was unmarked, warm and pink, and his chest moved with the ventilator. The nurses talked to him, knowing that hearing may be present even in the absence of all response. They tried hard to raise our hopes after the doctors' foreboding.

That evening his girlfriend arrived and she and my wife sat up with him all night while I went home and returned the next day with his elder brother. There was no change, only the news that blood had been taken for tissue typing. The implication did not escape us.

We went out for a walk and toyed with a token lunch while he was reassessed. On our return we were told unequivocally that there was no hope of survival and I was invited to examine the findings myself. I appreciated the offer but declined with thanks. I was a father, not a doctor, just then.

. The surgeon from the renal unit at St Mary's was on his way. We sat beside the body that was our beloved son, brother and boyfriend. There was this uncanny feeling about the scene. A few minutes earlier Nic was at least in one sense alive and there was hope. Now, although nothing had changed, he was dead and there was not hope. Yet so many signs of life continued, heartbeat, colour, respiration, albeit by ventilator, and warmth, although we noticed that his body was being allowed to cool.

The transplant surgeon arrived. He was very kind and said that there was an acute shortage of corneas as well as kidneys. We asked him to arrange for anything of value to be taken and said we had no hang-ups about beating heart donors. Keep him going as long as would be useful. I signed the appropriate piece of paper and we went to say goodbye to our Nic.

We made ourselves realise that all was not hopeless. Somewhere out there two people in renal failure would have the hope of their lives fulfilled and two who were blind would see. I wanted to say a few words of tribute and Christian hope over him, but all I could force out with rapidly vanishing self-control was the wish that those who lived with his kidneys and saw through his eyes might lead long and happy lives.

Then for the first time since childhood my cultivated composure disintegrated and I wept loudly and openly and cared not who heard and saw. My wife managed better and said a prayer of thanks for his life over him. We thanked the nurses, collected a pathetic bundle of clothes and went home.

How do I feel? I could never have forecast my immediate reactions. I no longer weep openly and although my emotions are noticeably more vulnerable, I have not become depressed. I miss Nic more than words can say and I cannot express how much the remaining youngsters mean to me. Even so, the family will never be complete again. He will never occupy his room, never take his place at table, nor sit down in our living room. I have only just begun to stop fantasising about him walking in the door as if nothing had ever happened.

Do I feel guilty about condoning his motorcycling? In his early teens it was I who gave him the job of cleaning the surgery, which unforeseen by me, gave him the means to start motorcycling independently of my support. Should we have banned the machine from our home? We decided to accept him with his youthful ambitions.

I am simply glad that there are no grounds for ill feeling about his death. To the last we never lost him and he died instantaneously doing what he most enjoyed.

How was Christmas? We knew Nic would have us enjoy the day, so at lunch we drank to his memory and celebrated as usual. Then the visitors went home, the youngsters went out, and we, his parents, wept in the lonely darkness. In January came his 21st birthday. We put flowers on his grave. It seemed such a futile gift as he had little interest in them when he was alive. Our wedding anniversary this year will be a hurdle. Nic would want us to celebrate the occasion that eventually gave rise to his conception, but no doubt the day will be spent quietly. Grief has drawn us even closer and perhaps anniversaries from now on will mean more to us as times of thought and reflection, instead of routine celebration.

I happen to be one of the many whose reaction to death is influenced by Christianity and non-religious parents may be interested in how this works.

I do not find the answers to the question, 'why Nic?' in religion, but in life. The first answer is in the counter-question 'why not Nic?' Secondly, I discover that freedom of all kinds entails risks and that means that the worst consequence, death, is going to happen to someone, sometime and by random chance, not with any form of fairness.

Freedom of speech, political freedom, freedom to climb mountains, to drive cars, and ride motorcycles costs lives. We gave Nic freedom and he paid the price and our loss is our share in that cost.

British Medical Journal
24 December 1983

Forewarned is Forearmed

Mother Frances Dominica SRN FRCN
Helen House, Oxford

I think it is helpful to warn parents or other newly bereaved people that other people's pious platitudes can be insensitive and hurtful; that however close the relationship between two people may be, they may grieve differently; and that the healing of grief is a very long, slow process. It is never complete; parents will never 'get over' the death of their child.

The pious platitudes are seemingly endless. 'Oh well, his sufferings are over now.' 'Poor little thing, it's a mercy really.' 'She is at peace.' 'Time will heal.' And worse follows, 'You're young enough to have another.' 'It's a good thing you've got the baby—that'll take your mind off it.' If there is someone to laugh with about these remarks it helps, and so too does the recognition that people want to be helpful and they do mean well. It's just that most people do feel inadequate and uncomfortable in the face of death and, if forced to say something, all sorts of things trip off the tongue.

Individuals grieve differently. For parents whose child has died there is the added complication that they are probably both worn down physically and emotionally, drained of the psychological resources they once had for meeting each other half way. One may grieve openly; the other finding it difficult to express grief. For both there will be an appalling vacuum at the centre of their lives, a sense of their arms being left empty. Half waking in the morning, the reflex of realisation that there is no child to tend. A whole empty day stretches ahead and the one left at home may envy the one who goes out to work, or sometimes vice versa. It can be painful putting on a cheerful face at work. However sympathetic colleagues or work mates may be initially, the continuing grief becomes uncomfortable for them. Taking the surviving child to playgroup or school, other parents tend to scatter as in the presence of one with a contagious disease. Sometimes the bereaved parent who takes most care with appearance or make up in a desperate attempt to 'put a face on it' and keep going is the one who gets least sympathy and support because he or she seems to be coping.

Parents and siblings may manifest grief in different ways. The overt grief, the crying, the sorrow, the reminiscing is easier to take than the pettiness, the short temper, the clinging behaviour of the children, the rows seemingly over nothing. It needs someone to say, 'It's all right. All these things are a very natural part of your grief. You haven't become a hateful person, neither has your husband, your wife, your child, your parent. Your anger against the doctor, the hospital, yourself, or God, is natural and safe.' Give it time. Hang on somehow. A day will come when you will wake up and think, yes, there is some point in being alive. And it needs a friend or friends, who will listen, however endlessly repetitious the conversation, who knows when to hug and when to stand back, who won't be offended by hurtful remarks, but will be alongside and readily available. Yet in all that I say about this and about all reactions and responses to death and bereavement, there are exceptions. We each have to be sensitive and to recognise that we may not be the right person and may not be acceptable alongside and that for some people grief is a private thing and must be respected as such.

For some, self-help groups such as *Compassionate Friends* or a support group such as *CRUSE* may be useful (see p.79). Those who have themselves experienced a similar type of bereavement can help as no one else can; the rest of us should guard against saying, 'I know how you feel'—we don't.

British Medical Journal
10 January 1987

3

The Thread Of Uncertainty

These days, a large percentage of the children who are diagnosed as having cancer can hope for a cure. Nonetheless, after accidents, cancer still remains the major cause of death in children under fifteen. With new treatments becoming available it is hoped that this situation will improve. The prospect of cure from childhood cancer has increased steadily over the last decade. Dr Judith Chessells, Haematology Consultant, states:
'About 60–70% of children with malignant disease can now expect to live a long time, even to be cured. So it has improved, not dramatically, but steadily, over the years, with the introduction of modern treatments.'

For some people, being told the diagnosis, that their child has cancer, is the worst time of all. It is almost as if their child died at that moment. In others there is often a feeling of unreality and disbelief; even denial.

Anger is also a strong emotion which can be inappropriately, although understandably, focused on the family doctor or the referring hospital. The doctors and other professionals working in the Cancer Unit, The Hospital for Sick Children, Great Ormond Street, London, feel that, however painful it may seem at the time, it is important to be honest with parents. Dr Judith Chessells:
'It's very painful to be frank with parents, to tell them that their child has a disease which is potentially fatal, and naturally they

are very distressed. But I think it's very important to be truthful, and we always try and share the truth with parents, even if it is painful, because I think there are more problems if you don't share the truth.'

Parents vary in the way they respond during their child's treatment. Some may go into a phase of mourning from the moment of diagnosis. Others may feel confident that their child will pull through. As the illness progresses, so a realisation is borne in, and grieving may begin halfway through the illness. With other parents, it is not until the child dies that the realisation hits home.

One of the most difficult things for a parent to live with is the uncertainty of not knowing whether their child will survive treatment. Even when a parent has been told that their child has a good chance, there is always the fear that treatment will fail.

The drugs involved in the treatment of cancer are powerful and often make the children very ill. It is stressful for both parents and staff to inflict further suffering on the child while in search of a cure. Because the nursing is highly technical, the nurses may not have as much time as they would like to get to know the children.

'You don't actually get as much time as you like to sit down and read them a story, play with them, because so much of your time is taken up with technical procedures.'

For the staff on the Unit, keeping the parents informed at every stage of their child's illness is especially important. In most cases, if the child is not responding well to treatment, their decline will be gradual, and the staff will work closely with the parents in deciding the best course to follow. In some cases, sadly, it is decided that chemotherapy treatment should be discontinued. Dr Jon Pritchard, Oncology Consultant:

'In a sense, it's the doctor's duty to make the decisions. But I think at the time the decision is made, it involves very careful and sensitive discussions with the family, and often with other relatives. You may need to have an input from grandparents sometimes, or an uncle, or an aunt who's particularly close; and from the GP, the paediatrician who's referred the child, social worker, psychologist and others, so that the best decision can be made for that particular family.'

When the decision has been made to stop the chemotherapy, the focus of the treatment changes and the aim is to give the best quality of life for the remaining period. With the careful use of drugs the child can generally be kept comfortable and pain-free.

When a child's death is imminent, parents need a lot of re-assurance from the medical team that nothing unexpected is going to happen and that their child will not die in great pain. Dr Peppy Brock:
'Sometimes it's a difficult balance to get it right, between giving them enough treatment, that they are not in pain, but that they also have contact with the family and that the family, in particular mum and dad, are there. And that even if they aren't reacting very much any more, they can feel a hand or hear a voice.'

It is not always possible to predict a child's death and very occasionally a child dies on the ward unexpectedly. This is far harder for a parent to cope with, because they have not had time to prepare themselves for the loss. It also has an immensely upsetting effect on the staff. Dr Richard Lansdown, Chief Psychologist:
'What is really hard for the ward staff is the sudden death. That really does come very rarely, but when it does come, there's always a reverberation around the ward for some time afterwards, and we have to pick up the pieces in some way.'

When it becomes likely that a child may die it is generally felt that to talk to the child honestly about their death is more helpful than to pretend that it is not going to happen. This is only done with the parents' consent. Children as young as four or five frequently have some idea of what death is, and for children up to the age of nine or ten, death can be talked about as a journey. The Great Ormond Street team felt that when children know that something is going to happen they can cope with it much more comfortably. Their greatest anxieties are about separation. Dr Richard Lansdown:
'"I don't mind dying, but I shall miss my mum and dad", is what one 4 year old said. And a number of children have expressed that anxiety. It's not the state of death, it's the fact they will no longer be with their loved ones.'

For the staff on the Unit, losing a child they have been caring

for over a period of time, is a very sad experience. It is important for them to be able to share their feelings of grief with each other and, to some extent, with the parents they will inevitably have grown close to over the period of caring for their child. Dr Judith Chessells:
'I can remember one terrible incident, where a child who I was very attached to, died, and the mother came back to speak to me and we were both in tears. And she was saying "Cheer up, doctor, *we're* alright, you've got to be alright." So I think one ought to be able to share one's feelings and show them that we're human.'

For the nurses who have been caring for the dying child on the ward it is vital for them to be able to say their last goodbyes:
'When a child dies on the ward, we tend to wash them and put them in their own clothes or in a gown. I feel quite privileged in being able to do that, and you can involve parents if they wish to be involved. I think for me it is a very important time in getting over the death of a child. It brings it home to me, that that's it. And I choose to do it on my own if I can, so that I can—I, too, can sort of say 'bye or cheerio to the child.'

Being Sensitive to Parents' Needs

Christa Müller

Sister Christa Müller has worked at The Hospital for Sick Children, Great Ormond Street, London, for 13 years. She is one of the longest serving members of the Cancer Unit team. She is currently working in the Outpatients Clinic.

We work very much as a team here in this hospital and I think it's always important that at the time of diagnosis a nurse is present when the consultant or the senior registrar tells the parents of their child's illness. All parents are different in the way they react and your role as a nurse is to sit and listen, and understand their particular needs. Very often parents are not able to take in much at the time of diagnosis and you have to explain to them again and again what has actually happened. I think it's very much the nurse's role to give support and let the parents know that they are not on their own and that, whatever the situation, we are available for the whole family throughout the treatment and afterwards.

I encourage parents to take each day at a time; and then each week at a time. Once they are at home they can perhaps start planning from month to month, but at the beginning only from day to day. Otherwise, the whole experience of hospitalisation, including chemotherapy and everything that goes with it would be too much to cope with.

I think the nurse who has actually been in the room at the time of diagnosis is really the nurse who's going to build up a relationship with the parents. And I think most probably that's the nurse that the parents will go back to and tell a little bit of what has been happening at home. You just share everything with the family in the end. They know quite a bit about you and you know a lot about them. What has happened doesn't just affect the patient, it affects everybody. It affects the grandparents, the close aunts, the frequent visitors to the house, and the neighbours and the school-friends.

I think when a consultant informs parents that their child is going to die, it is important that there is somebody available who has a good relationship with this family; who knows the details about the child and how the parents feel. The news may come as a shock, but most probably they will have had some idea and discussed it at home. It is important to go through the implications step-by-step and help them reach any decisions about treatment they may have to make.

I think a lot of parents fear the suggestion that their child's treatment be discontinued. It is important for the parents to know where they stand. Some parents may feel continuation of treatment is vital at all costs. Others that their children do not carry on with treatment, and that they enjoy the remainder of their lives at home. We just need to listen and be sensitive and see what the parents want us to do. Very often we make no decision at all on the day the parents are told, but let them go home. We then see them a few days later or whenever they are ready to discuss it again.

Parents should always be given the choice either to keep their child in hospital or to care for them at home. It very much depends on each family's situation as to which option best suits them. If they are very young parents, and it's the first death they have experienced in their lives, I think it must be very hard. They may feel more secure with hospital care and if so, that's certainly the right place for their child. If they have very good community care with a nurse available at all times and they know they won't be on their own, then perhaps home is the right place for them. But one has to give them space to talk about it and let them know what is available. Some parents don't want to care for their child at home because of brothers and sisters; they may feel it's just too much. Other parents are worried about pain, and are afraid that pain cannot be controlled at home. It is important that, given the facilities available, parents are allowed to make a choice.

When a child is dying on the ward it is important that the parents are not left on their own if they need support. If they prefer to be alone then that's fine; and the nurses should be available when needed. Many parents would rather have somebody sitting with them. It is important to respect what parents want. If they want their child to be in a cubicle, then that's where the child should be. If they prefer their child to be in the open ward because they know all the children on the ward and they want their child to be with them, then that's what should happen. But most of the time the children are in a cubicle because they want to be quiet and asleep rather than having noise and television around them. Again, there's no set rule about it and we need to be sensitive and see what the parents' wishes are and if at all possible, to grant those wishes.

4

Cheryl

Rose and Ken discovered that their 5 year old daughter, Cheryl, had cancer on her third birthday when a series of X-rays showed up a lump in her abdomen. It was neuroblastoma, a type of cancer largely confined to children and very resistant to treatment. Cheryl underwent ten courses of chemotherapy and surgery, but eventually the tumour regrew.

Doctors at The Hospital for Sick Children, Great Ormond Street, London, offered the possibility of more treatment, but advised that Cheryl was unlikely to survive.

After a great deal of thought and discussion with doctors and relatives, Rose and Ken chose not to go ahead with further treatment. They felt in the light of Cheryl's poor prognosis, they could not justify putting her through any further pain and discomfort.

Rose and Ken then had another decision to make—whether to keep Cheryl in hospital, with all the available professional expertise, or whether to take her home and care for her in the warmth of the family. Cheryl had become increasingly unsettled in hospital and the time spent away from home was having a negative effect on their other 6 year old daughter, Stephanie.

Rose and Ken decided to take Cheryl home. In making this decision, one of their greatest concerns was keeping her free from pain. Because her tumour had spread, she required a lot of medication. Rose felt:

'We didn't want her to be in pain. So long as we keep her at home and she's not in pain, I think that's the best place for her.'

The Symptom Care Team at Great Ormond Street Hospital were able to provide reassurance. This team, run by a doctor and two nurses, offered them the professional support necessary to keep Cheryl at home and generally free of pain. It has been recently set up with private funding to provide support in such circumstances and it is not a service that is available in all hospitals. A nurse from the team, working in conjunction with the local GP, and liaising with the local hospital, advised the family on nursing and medication. She also offered counselling for the parents in dealing with the difficulties in caring for their child at home.

Rose and Ken knew that they could take Cheryl into Great Ormond Street or the local hospital at any time, and that their local GP was available to write prescriptions and to answer questions. Dr Jones, their GP, felt they had made the right decision: 'I would always feel that, if possible, anyone should have the right to die at home, provided, of course, that the people looking after them are capable of coping with the physical and emotional problems that arise. I think, on the whole, a good loving family would always try to have their children with them right to the end.'

Having Cheryl at home enabled Rose to look after the rest of the family, as well as attend to Cheryl's needs:
'She doesn't eat at regular dinner times, so you give her what she wants any time. Even during the night we're up with her giving her things to eat. If you were in hospital you wouldn't be able to do that.'

Stephanie was much happier with Cheryl at home. And Ken felt that they could live more as a family since Cheryl had returned home and, in particular, Stephanie had benefited:
'Stephanie likes it. She looks after Cheryl every time she comes home from school. She reads her a story, or colours with her. You know, she looks after her. She's always sitting next to her and helping her. And I think she really likes it.'

At first Rose and Ken didn't find it easy to talk to Cheryl about

dying, but after taking advice from Great Ormond Street Hospital they started to raise this with her:
'We just said to Cheryl that, "You'll be going to heaven, and it's a nice place to go. There'll be other children to play with, and lots of flowers and grass, and you won't have to take your tablets and you won't be in any pain".'
They were pleased to find that Cheryl accepted their explanation and seemed reassured. Stephanie, too, was involved in the conversation and wondered if she and her parents were also going to heaven. Rose explained to her that because of Cheryl's illness, God wanted her now and that the rest of the family would be following her later on.

Dr Richard Lansdown, Chief Psychologist at Great Ormond Street, feels it is important to be honest as far as possible with children:
'Children as young as four and five frequently have a good idea of what death is all about and so we must approach them initially with some respect for their understanding.'

Parents whose children have been dying over a period of time have to some extent been able to work through their loss and say their goodbyes. What has been important for Rose and Ken is having Cheryl at home and being able to care for her within the family. As Rose says:
'We've come to terms with the fact that she's going to die. It could be any time, so really we're just waiting and keeping her comfortable.'

Rose and Ken looked after Cheryl at home until the day before her death.

She died in hospital on February 22nd, 1987.

A Short Life

John Killingback

Our daughter Emma was only 27 months old when we learned she had cancer. She had an appointment at our local hospital for a small hernia. A few days before we went, Carole's mother, who was babysitting for us, noticed a 'lump' on her back. So when we saw the consultant we asked him to look at the lump and he told us Emma was a 'very sick child'. Carole said, 'does she have cancer?' He said 'Yes, I'm afraid she does'.

It's difficult to express how we felt at that moment. We were in such shock—so upset and very afraid. But we didn't want to let Emma see how we were feeling. Arrangements were made for us to go immediately to Great Ormond Street Hospital. I had to drive, trying not to cry and finding it hard to concentrate. All I could think of was that our lovely daughter had cancer and that she might die.

Waiting for the tests to come through to show what kind of cancer Emma was suffering from and whether or not it might be treatable, was one of the longest weekends I've ever known. And when the results came, they were bad. Emma had a Stage IV neuroblastoma; she had at best a 20% chance of survival.

Emma started on a course of chemotherapy which it was hoped would shrink the tumour and make it more operable. It was very distressing for her. The drugs made her vomit continuously and within 3 weeks all her beautiful blond curls began to fall out. Unfortunately, the chemotherapy failed to shrink the tumour but, despite the danger, it was decided to go ahead and operate. I remember a nurse taking Emma down to the theatre. She was calling for her mummy. We knew we might never see her again.

Although Emma made a quick recovery from the operation, being allowed home after 4 days, she was soon complaining of tummy pains and we had to take her back to Great Ormond Street. Tests showed nothing and at first it was suggested that maybe Emma's tummy pains were just an attempt to get attention. To our great regret we listened to the staff and not to Emma. We so much wanted her to be better. But a few days later another tumour was discovered. The consultant told us that there was no further treatment that could be given to cure Emma and suggested that she might be better off in the familiar surroundings of her own home.

We thought Emma had a couple of months to live but in fact it was only one. It was so hard to watch her die. Neither Carole nor I had ever experienced death, let alone the death of our little daughter. We worried about how our son would cope with the loss of his sister. Most of all we worried about how she would die. The only way to stop her pain was to dose her with morphine. We could do nothing else to help.

In desperation, but not faith, we brought in a faith-healer and also took a trip to Lourdes. Our time in Lourdes was precious, not just because we had only a few days left with Emma, but because we were completely alone, just our small family, sharing that last time together.

Back at home we were fortunate to have a daily visit from the nurses of a local hospice where Emma could have gone. They supplied the drugs necessary to stop her pain.

Towards the end she was so full of morphine that she was almost in a coma, unable to communicate with us. But we were pleased that she could stay at home. She died in my arms on January 8th 1986, aged just 2 years 11 months.

Soon after Emma's death, we decided we should like to start a fund in her name, to research into a cure for neuroblastoma. We felt this might give her short life an extra meaning, other than the evident joy and love she gave us, so in conjunction with the *Neuroblastoma Society*, we started the *Emma Killingback Memorial Fund*.

Trusting Instinct

Mother Frances Dominica SRN FRCN
Helen House, Oxford

One beautiful autumn day a 10 month old baby boy died. We knew that he could not live very long, but his actual death came on a day when he seemed particularly alert and happy. When he died his mother carried him into the garden, walked and sat with him in her arms for a couple of hours, often with one of us beside her, occasionally alone with him. She cried gently and talked to him. She remembered the day he was born, also a beautiful sunny day; she talked of all the joy that he had brought into life and of the pain.

Then in her own time she carried him back into their room and lay down with him still in her arms and slept for an hour. Then, and only then, was she ready to wash and dress him with very great love and care and without any sense of hurry. She chose the clothes he was to wear and the toys he was to have with him. She had already seen the small room, furnished much like a bedroom, but able to be kept very cold, where he was to lie for the next few days. She carried him there. The little boy's mother and father visited him often in that small room, sometimes brushing his hair or rearranging his toys, sometimes lifting him out of his cot and sitting with him, uncurling his fingers and looking again at his hands, kissing him in the nape of his neck, lost in grief and the wonder of the miracle that was their son. All they needed was our permission, spoken or unspoken, to do it their way, the way they knew instinctively, and our presence in the background and the knowledge that we felt pain and wonder too and were not afraid to show it.

As we cope with life, so will we cope with death. Difficulties and conflict in relationships in the ordinary course of events may not disappear in the presence of death, indeed in the midst of distress they may be painfully exaggerated. It is not for those of us who are involved professionally to take sides, but rather to believe the best of each individual and to try to support without discrimination. One relative may remain dry-eyed and controlled throughout; the other hysterical and seemingly out of control. We have to accept both and not be thrown off balance by either. To whom is the hysterical reaction of a newly bereaved teenager a threat? In the privacy of a room can that young person not be allowed to lie down beside the dead brother or sister or hold the child or scream to God to bring this person he or she loves back to life again? And if that teenager asks to be left alone with the dead child for a time, can we not take the risk? All this may be an essential part in the whole process of healing. Each member of the family, not just the chief mourner, has a right and a need to grieve and express that grief in his or her own way.

British Medical Journal
10 January 1987

5

Life Sentence

Every year in Great Britain, over 30 children are murdered. We examine how the parents of murdered children may also become victims of the crime.

For the families involved, feelings of grief and anger are compounded by the intrusion of the media and the inevitable police investigation that follows. For a few days, they are both headline news and, worse still, on the list of suspects.

Unlike the child's murderer they have no chance of remission, no parole for good behaviour. They live for the rest of their lives with the knowledge of the way their child died.

Ann's son Andrew was murdered on his way to a youth club. His body was found stabbed, strangled and mutilated in a derelict house the following day. Because of the way he died, Ann's grief was overwhelming:

'You can't believe the fact that they've died. The shock of that is bad enough. But to think that something so terrible has happened to your child, that child you've protected all the years, nurtured, looked after. I kept thinking he must have cried out for us and we weren't there. And it leaves you so helpless, inadequate, you've failed and to think what he went through—I just can't come to terms with it even now. It was just horrible.'

Families find the pain and suffering connected with the murder especially difficult to deal with. The anger and pain that they experience dominates their emotions for a very long time. They find they can think of nothing else. The mental imagery is acute and places an enormous strain on their emotional well-being.

June and John's daughter, Tracy, was murdered 11 years ago and the murderer has still not been caught. After all these years John would still like revenge for his daughter's death.

'Over the years I've sort of quietened down my thoughts, but if I had him in front of me now I would willingly rip him to pieces. And I'm not a violent person at all. . . . I wouldn't be satisfied until he was absolutely dead one hundred per cent.'

Wendy and John's daughter, Samantha, was murdered while on an exchange trip to France when she was eighteen. They heard of her death in the early hours of the morning when a policeman knocked on the door and handed them a note.

'A few days before she was due to come home we got a note in the night. The police knocked on the door about three in the morning with a memo, saying "Passport Number so and so murdered on the riverbank", and that was it.'

Daphne and Joyce's children Robert and Michele were brutally murdered one Saturday afternoon by a work colleague. They were seventeen. Daphne was horrified when the Police treated her as one of the suspects:

'We were all in the same room at the beginning and I felt really threatened by the police. I didn't like their attitude. Since then I understand they've got to be like that because we may be guilty. But you don't think that way. We would no more think of murdering our kids than fly in the air.'

Yet, according to statistics, 7 out of 10 child murders are committed by parents or 'co-habitees'. So the police have a difficult task in confronting the bereaved parents. They have to extract the necessary facts whilst being sensitive to the parents' grief.

The Metropolitan Police train their officers in the difficult task of delivering bad news to parents or other relatives. Chief Inspector Paul Mathias of the Metropolitan Police Training College, Hendon:

'We can all sympathise with people (in this situation). But to actually empathise, to actually understand it from the other person's position, to understand the sort of torment they are going through really requires a particular input. And that's why we have been keen to ensure that all our officers are receiving this particular component in their training.'

Parents become obsessed with the desire to find out everything about the case and often want precise details of how their child died. The Police generally try to keep this information from them, hoping to spare their feelings. They usually advise parents against seeing the child's body in case it will upset them more. However, many parents want to see and touch the child's body, no matter how badly mutilated, so they can say their last goodbye. Ann Robinson:

'I knew that I wanted to see Andrew and kiss him goodbye. And, in fact, his coffin was sealed and I was asked not to see him. And not being in any emotional state to make a firm decision, I allowed myself to be guided not to see him. I'm sure people did it for the best reasons, but, in retrospect, it would have been better if I'd seen him.'

There are no guidelines for the press on coverage of child murders. A crime reporter from a leading newspaper talks about how journalists approach this situation:

'We have to balance our job as a professional journalist, with our own feelings as a parent and a human being. We are in the market for selling newspapers, so obviously we want to get the best story we possibly can, but in the end we are human beings, we are citizens. We have to live with our consciences afterwards.'

For Joyce, this 'balance' was not immediately evident. She had reporters hounding her day and night:

'My boy tried to get an injunction out, but the police said, you can't unless they're outside your door all the time. They were stopping neighbours, asking what sort of girl Michele was. They were at my firm wanting to know why I wasn't at work. And one of the women who works with me said to them "Why do you want to know this? You're trying to pull the girl to pieces".'

The way the press and television handle the subject of child murders is one issue currently being considered by the working party of the *National Association of Victim Support Schemes* (p.86).

Their director, Helen Reeves, talks about the problems of the parents of murdered children, a group who, until now, have often been neglected.

'One of the issues is that parents themselves, or the families themselves, haven't been identified as a group, and therefore they're all isolated. They're on their own, in their own homes. They have neighbours and friends, but nobody has really identified this wide need, particularly in the city areas where it's happening a lot. There are beginning to be a number of small groups, like victim support, who will be able to help, to make sure that everybody's aware of the need.'

But the media are not alone in their insensitivity. The parent of a murdered child often feels isolated in a world where very few people around them understand their torment, or are willing to share their feelings. Even GPs often back away from parents because they feel insufficiently trained to cope. Ann Robinson says of her GP:

'He didn't really seem to have enough time to sit and talk to me, which is what I wanted, or to sit and listen to me. So he did what he felt was the thing he could do best, I suppose. He just got out the old prescription pad and more sleeping tablets, more tranquillisers.'

Friends and relatives can be equally unresponsive. Often, for the parents of murdered children, it is only when they meet others who have been through the same experience that they begin to feel that their unhappiness is neither abnormal nor insane. Ann Robinson:

'People, family and friends, they avoid talking about Andrew, because they think it's going to upset me, or it's going to remind me. That's ridiculous, I don't need reminding. He's in my thoughts all the time. And I've got very, very distressed on many occasions when I try to introduce him into the conversation and the subject was changed, or there'd be an embarrassed silence. I can remember screaming, literally screaming, "I had Andrew, he was alive, he was here for nearly fourteen years. Talk about him!"

The Response to Violent Death

Dr Colin Murray Parkes
Senior Lecturer in Psychiatry
London Hospital Medical College

Research has shown that deaths which are sudden, unexpected and untimely, commonly give rise to a type of grieving that can only be regarded as pathological. In the short term, psychic numbing and disbelief may help to protect the bereaved from extreme distress and enable them to come through an emergency situation. But as time passes it becomes clear that the very success of these psychological defences is making it hard for the bereaved to complete the task of mourning.

This task may be even more difficult if the death is particularly horrific, if there is no chance to see the body, or if there is particular reason for intense feelings of anger or guilt.

In such instances it is common for bereaved people to remain excessively anxious and withdrawn. They may cling to unrealistic fantasies that the dead will return, or remain trapped in a state of chronic self-punitive grief. Two, three, and four years later many will be coping less well with their roles and responsibilities than other bereaved people and they continue to pine for the lost person and to miss them intensely.

There is much that can be done by members of the caring professions to help people through these difficult times. Many disasters cast their shadow before, and there are sometimes opportunities to help people to prepare themselves for a coming suicide or one of those 'accidental' deaths which come of alcoholism or other self-destructive behaviour.

The impact of violent death can be mitigated if the news is broken as gently and tactfully as possible. Adequate practical and emotional support is essential and people must be given time to react to the news and to ask questions. Viewing of the body requires sensitive handling, but should in general be encouraged.

The rites of the church help to bring home the significance of what has happened. They draw together people who can support the bereaved and they enable people of common faith to find meaning in the face of death. If performed with proper preparation and sympathy, they can become a personal tribute to the dead and a source of comfort to the bereaved.

During the early stages after a death the bereaved sometimes reject offers of help for fear their defences will not be respected. But those who are willing to accept help will benefit greatly from opportunities to vent their feelings of bewilderment, distress, rage and self-reproach.

People may need permission and encouragement to grieve. But there also comes a time when they need permission and encouragement to stop grieving. Violent deaths violate our confidence in the order of things. It may be a long time before the bereaved again begin to trust in others and longer still before they are prepared to run the risk of loving another person. Yet it is often the love and care of other people that will get them through.

The Special Needs of Families of Murdered Children

Ann Robinson, National Co-ordinator
Parents of Murdered Children Support Group (p.87)

The *Parents of Murdered Children Support Group* was formed within *Compassionate Friends* when a number of parents of murdered children, including myself, began to identify a very specific need to meet others who had experienced the same form of isolation and grief.

Families who share this tragedy can give each other great emotional support, and the group has proved invaluable in this respect. But the group has brought to light a real need for informed practical help. On top of the deep grief felt by the parents, which is intensified by the sheer horror of the way their children have died, they have to cope with additional traumas, such as the intrusion of the media, police investigations and the trial. Very few parents have the 'know how' or the contacts to deal with these legal and procedural issues.

Because of the shock, anger and the time-lapse before a trial, skilled bereavement/family counselling is often needed, but is rarely available. Nobody from the 'caring agencies' automatically offers support to families, and consequently they feel let down by a society that mostly leaves them to cope alone.

As Co-founder and Co-ordinator of the group, I contacted several statutory and voluntary agencies, looking for help. But the answer was usually a stunned silence followed by 'So sorry, but we're not really qualified to help. . .'

Helen Reeves, Director of the *National Association of Victims Support Schemes* (NAVSS), is aware that more work is necessary to aid families of murder victims. Some local victims support schemes were already being supportive, but others felt too daunted to become involved.

Helen met us to discuss the problems that members of the group were experiencing. She explained how NAVSS decided that help was needed from more than one source, and identified the agencies who would be involved initially with parents. Representatives from the police, a victims support scheme, *Compassionate Friends* and *CRUSE* were invited to form a working party under the guidance of the NAVSS.

The purpose of the working party is to allow agencies to combine their resources and make recommendations on how support for families of murdered victims may be improved.

The working party recommends that the police refer all murder cases to the victims support scheme, who will provide a trained person to give support and practical help in liaising with the police, the press, the Criminal Injuries Compensation Board, and the courts. They will also link-up with medical and counselling services and other self-help organisations, such as *Compassionate Friends*, to help families on a long term basis.

6

Suicide

Graham's daughter Sonja died in May 1986; she was 16 years old. After 2 years of ill-health she became depressed and took an overdose of the anti-depressants she was prescribed. Graham:
'I know nothing else could ever happen in my life which could be worse than what has happened. I could face anything now.'

Graham, his wife Dorothy and son Stephen talked to us about how they have faced what has happened and why. Their 'what ifs' are endless.

Three and a half years ago Peter and Iris lost both their sons. Graham, 18, and Christopher, 14, drove their car into high bracken, connected a hose pipe from the exhaust into the car and started the engine. Peter and Iris will never know why. Their sons' bodies were found the next morning. They talk here about how they've lived through the last 3 years. Iris.
'Really, it's too big, too big a thing to think about. You just don't believe it will ever happen to you, and I think this is why you close your eyes to some of the things they said, because at the end of the day, we never believed it would happen.'
Peter:
'In some respects, maybe an accident, we could have accepted a little more, not easily, no child's death is easy, I don't mean that, but it's unnatural this way. Completely unnatural.'
Peter and Iris needed to come to terms with Graham and Christopher's deaths in different ways. Peter:

'Iris used to go over and over, I think basically searching for the answer, which I don't think we'll get, anyway in this world. My tendency is to try and hide behind a wall. It's a very thin wall, a fragile wall easily broached. But if I can stay behind it I can deal with it. If it's broached, which Iris does sometimes, I'm afraid I go down and get upset and hurt. It's just too much for me to take.'

Dorothy and Graham each have their own mechanisms for dealing with Sonja's death. Dorothy:
'Graham likes to back off and reflect. And I can get a bit panicky about that sometimes. But then you have to say "I'll go along with that". If it's got to the point where I can't take it any more I've said that to him and he was there.'
Graham feels he can cope better if he stops looking for reasons why:
'You can't find the answer, you drive yourself crackers if you continue to search, because we'll never be able to answer it.'

Peter still finds every day is a fight:
'I still have my down moments, I still cry, but in the passage of time I can talk about it more. I accept it more and it does get a bit easier. It never leaves you. I don't think it will ever leave us.'

For Iris, mornings are the worst.
'It still hits me now, every day, about what's happened. I'm just waiting for the morning when I don't wake up and think about it.'

Dorothy:
'It's this overwhelming feeling, right or wrong that parents are there to protect their children. To do the best for them, to help them grow up.'

Graham:
'You feel as though you've let that child down badly. We endeavour to bring our children up in a open happy atmosphere, and obviously it wasn't enough.'

Dorothy:
'What do you say when your daughter says "what's the meaning of life?" She's saying "you've had difficult times, what brought you through?" And you sense how important it is that you say

something that means something to them. She did know we cared. She did know we were trying. It wasn't enough.'

Sonja's brother Stephen, was 14 years old when she died. He was very close to her and in the year before she died she confided in him about how unhappy she was. After her death he tried to deal with it in his own way. He felt he might have made the wrong decision in respecting her trust in him by not telling Graham and Dorothy how she felt. Dorothy:
'There was a look of tension and panic about him. His eyes were everywhere in his head. He couldn't stand still and talk. And as the days went on I could see he was getting more and more tired. I was very concerned . . . and I was aware that he didn't want to talk about it.'
They were determined not to have a repetition of what had happened to Sonja and eventually managed to find support from a professional counsellor. They found that not only Stephen, but the whole family needed help. Dorothy:
'Counselling isn't a magic wand. It doesn't make it easier and less painful. It just focuses the family's need to talk to each other and be open, and say the bad feelings as well as the good ones. If counselling's not for you, don't give up. Talk to each other.'

Peter and Iris also found it is important to talk, not just to each other but also to other people. Iris:
'Right from the beginning, the first day—when we knew they were gone—we were always glad when someone came to see us. It really does help.'

Bereavement Counselling

A personal view from Dorothy

It is said 'Time is a great healer'. Maybe it is—eventually. For us it was no help to be told this when we were so distraught over the loss of Sonja.

I suppose it is quite normal that the shock and grief meant we all behaved erratically for a few weeks. But after 5 or 6 weeks I felt a growing concern, and eventually alarm at what was happening. Stephen was still unable to stay in the house for more than the time it took to eat meals or change clothes. He did not talk much at all, was dark under his eyes, pale and anxious. He slept only fitfully, jumping up in the night and crying out. Graham, my husband, was withdrawn, uncommunicative and always tired. Though Graham had always had times when he was quiet and reflective, I just *knew* this was not the same.

This all may sound perfectly normal in the circumstances; probably just my own anxiety. My GP, he confirmed this in a round-about sort of way. More weeks passed and nothing changed. My concern for Stephen grew—he was exhausted and bereft and I didn't know what to do. More 'phone calls to the GP, even a visit saw no response. 'Everything was normal' or 'only to be expected in the circumstances'.

I decided to search for other sources of help, mostly by telephoning every organisation I could think of. The social services sent someone round from the *Crisis Intervention Team*. He talked to Stephen a few times and myself once. He seemed reluctant to refer us on. After more telephoning and being passed on, or told no help was available, I finally heard of the *Child Guidance Centre*. They agreed that Stephen needed help and informed me that the whole family would be seen together. My GP agreed to refer us and at last I felt we could get some support.

Graham was particularly reluctant to go at first, but then decided we could hardly expect Stephen to go if he did not show willing.

We have been having sessions, usually lasting an hour, for almost 9 months now. Stephen has had several sessions by himself, but is also present for the family sessions. In these we talk about Sonja, ourselves and our concerns about each other. Sometimes when one of us says 'Oh, everything's been much better' or 'I feel fine' another family member will prompt that it has not seemed that way to them.

Having sessions as a family has been really very helpful. We discovered we *all* felt bad about enjoying ourselves sometimes. That each of us feels just as guilty about certain things we did or said, or didn't do or say which just might have prevented Sonja's suicide. Each of us also had the opportunity to remind each other of the many things we did do to help. Our counsellor was able to offer both reassurance and guidance or information which was most helpful when we felt so uncertain. For example our fears for Stephen were very intense and we were not applying our usual house rules: we had become very lax and were letting him do things we wouldn't normally allow. Through counselling we learned this could have added to a sense of insecurity, when he most needed to feel secure. We became aware that this was all part of our parental reaction and grief.

Time, to grieve and talk, is what has helped us—not just time itself. We are more open now about our feelings of loss. Sometimes just sharing happy memories with pleasure. It has been a very gradual process but one which has taken us nearer to normal family life, not a pretense because of held back feelings or trying to 'protect' each other. It is now clear that the sharing, being open and the gentle support of our counsellor, has helped us enormously in this process.

A Letter From Jill

On 28th December 1984, Jill died, aged 15 years, on the Liverpool to Manchester railway line. She told her parents she was taking the dog for a walk, tied him in a safe place and threw herself under a train. She left a letter.

Dear Mummy,

Please don't waste too much effort on a large funeral after all the heartache I have caused you, it is hardly worth it. I am sorry it happened at Christmas. I killed myself because I had made a mess of so many things.

I know you feel that that isn't true, but it was. It was

never your fault, mind. I love you and Daddy very dearly, always remember that. I could just not get the act together, that's all. My future didn't seem very attractive. I think I was just one hell of a cracked-up person. I have always felt inferior. I could never talk to anyone and know they had respected what I have said. Maybe I didn't let it show before because then I was younger and adulthood seemed a long way away and I thought as I got older my thoughts would change. Sadly they didn't.

Always remember me as you thought I was, not as a stupid person, which is how I feel about myself.

I can't not kill myself after writing this. (Sorry)

Love, Jill xxxx

Your disobedient daughter

Nigel

At the age of 14, Nigel began to feel lonely and isolated. His mother had died when he was 8 years old and his suppressed grief led him to feel suicidal. Fortunately, he managed to find professional help. At his lowest he found comfort in writing:

I run all day
I run all night
So many things to say
So many reasons to fight

I smile with you
yet I cry on my own.
All laughs are a farce
And all the smiles are skin deep
the moods never pass
You're in my dreams when I sleep

I can't see why
I can't see what it's about
I don't know why I cry
I just can't work it out

The Problem Of Suicide

Every year 4000 people take their own lives. One every two hours. It's the most common cause of death in teenagers after road accidents.

Twenty thousand people every year attempt suicide. Hospitals are treating some 2000 young people—usually drug overdoses—every week and the number is rising.

Assistant Director of the mental health charity *MIND*, Ron Lacey, tells us:
'Adolescents tend to feel things much more intensely than at any time before or after in their lives. They are struggling with their adult social identity and any failure, in love or exams, is much more significant to them.

Youngsters need to take risks and rebel and test limits. A parent has to judge when to leave well alone. But parents should never blame themselves entirely for their children's problems. Circumstances may affect a child but he or she also has a will.'

The *Samaritans* supply a list of danger signs for parents to look for in their children:
• teenager's inability to relate to them
• a definite idea of how to commit suicide
• the giving away of possessions
• dependence on alcohol or drugs.

It is not true that those who talk about it don't do it. Suicide attempts are rarely simply hysterical cries for help, and many may, and do, try again.

A study by psychiatrists in Oxford gives us an insight into which young people are most vulnerable and those most likely to adjust. Girls turn to the pill bottle when facing a passing problem. Boys think of suicide only when trapped by a number of persistent problems and then reject the idea of an overdose as unmanly. Surprisingly, three clear groups emerged:

1   Children whose problem had bothered them for less than a month before the overdose tended to be younger, lived with one or both parents and had never seen a psychiatrist before. They had problems relating to individuals rather than to their family or society. Most claimed to have bad relationships with their fathers.

They were most likely to say that they wouldn't ever try suicide again and didn't need further help.

2   Children whose problems had existed for more than a month also mostly lived with their parents and were more likely to have been depressed in the past, to have more difficulty relating to parents and feel isolated, although they claimed to have friends.

Counselling over a long period seemed to help.

3   Children who had problems for over a month and had also been in trouble for something like stealing or truancy were likely to have lived with foster parents or other relatives. Taking an overdose was just one more anti-social act.

Counselling didn't appear to help and researchers feared this group were at risk of later successful suicide.

For young people seeking help the first stop can always be the doctor. But if he or she isn't helpful, school counsellors or social services may help. Counselling organisations are listed on p.78.

For parents *Compassionate Friends* has an SOS group with a dual name, *The Shadow of Suicide/Survivors of Suicide*, which puts parents who have lost children through suicide in touch with each other.

7

Catherine

Catherine Dunbar died, when she was 22 years old, of anorexia. She left behind diaries and letters which formed the basis of the book *Catherine: The Story of a Girl who Died from Anorexia Nervosa*, written by Catherine's mother Maureen Dunbar (Viking Books, 1986). Extracts from the book are reproduced here by kind permission of Penguin Books Ltd.

Catherine began life with eating difficulties which later developed into anorexia. The illness first began to manifest itself when, in 1976, Catherine's father had serious business problems and the family was under a great deal of strain, having to move home several times. That summer she was unsettled and with another move imminent, she went to boarding school. In January the following year Catherine's head mistress rang her mother to say that Catherine had ceased eating. After consultation Catherine was admitted to hospital for the first time. She was then only 15 years old.

10 March 1978

I want to be 6 st 7 lb this is a large problem.

I feel fed up and depressed with life sometimes.
I feel like c.s. (committing suicide). It is my

faith in God that stops me doing it for He gave me
life and it would be the devil that would make me
take it away. I don't want that because I don't
follow the devil but God.

I can't explain to anyone exactly how I feel
because they wouldn't understand. I feel a burden
to everyone and I have been for a year. I wish to
God I didn't feel like this. I'd give anything in
the world to be a natural, sane girl, but it
doesn't seem meant for me yet. . . . I am too
depressed again and I feel insecure. I am
obsessed with my weight. . .

. . . I want to take my Os in November and please God
I'll succeed at them, if nothing else in life. I
just want to hide from people and life and
uncertainty. How can I overcome it? It is an
impossible task all alone.

From *Catherine*
p.32

Catherine had always been finicky with food, but now this
gradually became an obsession. She craved food constantly, but
her mind rejected it. She felt guilty and unclean. She became
totally preoccupied with cooking. She would prepare large
meals for the family, but would refuse to sit at the table with
them to eat. If anyone walked in the room while she was eating
she would either panic and protest or she would pretend she had
not been eating. The only time she swallowed solid food was
during a binge. At other times she would chew food, then re-
move it from her mouth and place it in a basin. When she wasn't
at home the basin was replaced by a secret plastic bag, or even her
pocket.

Routine was desperately important. Her 'eating' occurred

three times a day at exactly the same time. If for any reason she was five minutes late for it, she would panic, cry and often not be able to touch it.

16 January 1982

Today was one of my worst days for a long time.
This morning I went into Croydon, Mummy drove me.
I bought a bathrobe and some magazines and then I
came home. This outing unsettled me because it is
not usual. This afternoon I was in mental agony.
I just felt like eating and bingeing. Bingeing is
the only way I have of remaining in my own world
and of being able to indulge in food, thus taking
my mind off everything, particularly my problems.
Vomiting uses up my mental and physical energy,
sometimes it leaves me hyperactive, but today it
left me feeling drowsy. I am so restless and
unhappy I cannot go on. I don't know what will
happen. I just know that I cannot face hospital.

From *Catherine*
p.62–63.

Catherine had been a high achiever, a perfectionist, who sat her 'O' levels, even in hospital. When she had jobs she was extremely good at them. She took a secretarial course and gained work in an export firm, but when her strength failed she had to resign. Amazingly, despite her illness she managed to hold down a job as a nanny caring for small children, until she became too weak to continue working.

As her anorexia took hold she found herself stealing food from shops—biscuits and chocolates—which she used to hoard. She also became addicted to laxatives, taking up to 140 a day. She feared and dreaded 'bingeing' which she carried out repeatedly. Here is her own record of such a binge.

26 June 1981

Mood: Abnormally cheerful
Weight: 31.3 kilos
Breakfast: Kit Kat and tea
Lunch: Tea, soda water, *Kit Kat*, 2 cinnamon, 1 cheese.
Supper: Tea, *Kit Kat*, 2 sausage rolls, spring greens, mashed potato (knowing I could binge later).
Binge: Spring greens, sausage rolls, potatoes (boiled and mashed), toast, apple pickings, cottage cheese pickings, *shreddies.*
Laxatives: 109 approximately morning and evening (work).
Remarks: Not too bad a day. I knew the family would be going out this evening about 9 o'clock so I had supper about 7.50 and then binged later when they were out. I felt quite cheerful today but deep down I feel a wave of depression and am waiting for it to break out. It could be a few days, one can never tell with me.

From *Catherine*
p.55

The bingeing caused blackouts and feelings of loathing and hatred towards herself. When her weight rose above the painfully low targets she set herself, she believed that she was fat, ugly and grotesque. Although she was devoutly religious, Catherine attempted to kill herself twice by overdosing.

Catherine hated the secretiveness and the way in which it had changed her so fundamentally. Her family, who tried their best to help Catherine, recognised two distinct sides to her. There was the loving, sweet natured, helpful Catherine and the selfish, demanding anorexic Catherine. Her father, John Dunbar related in *Catherine* (p.129):

'I remember my lack of understanding that such a logical intelli-

gent girl could do this to herself; my sheer anger, intolerance and
frustration, which I used to voice to her in an effort to shake her
off the fatal course. I tried logic, bribery, threats and pleading
with her, even though it upset her. I had to keep on trying in the
hope that any change of emotion might arouse her desire and
will to fight to live.

All that I did or said was the best I could do at the time in those
circumstances. My logical mind could not comprehend, but
sadly there is no logic in anorexia. There will always be a deep
feeling of extreme failure, sorrow and pain for the loss of a lovely
daughter with an illness no one fully understands. I loved her
dearly.'

During the last 2 weeks of her life Catherine suffered intolerable
pain. She never admitted it, yet the suffering was clear from her
face and she was constantly crying out in agony while she was
asleep.

On 2nd January 1984, she died of starvation, aged 22.

A Plea To Professionals

Maureen Dunbar

Jacqueline is 19 years old and a student at Cambridge. She has
been, until recently, totally confined to bed (her bed pan removed by a male nurse). At present she is allowed up, but not to
get dressed. She spends the day in her night clothes. She has
nothing with which to fill her time during the long daylight
hours. She has a great love of literature, but is denied her books.
Her family and friends have been told not to visit her. Is this a
case for the court of human rights? No—Jacqueline's 'crime' is to
have anorexia.

I am happy to say not all hospitals mete out this treatment.
Unhappily many still do.

I am not a member of the medical profession, I am not a professional of any kind. I am merely the mother of a girl who had anorexia nervosa and who subsequently died of it. I lived through 7 years of Catherine's agony, and seeing my family almost destroyed.

In hindsight, I can see the mistakes made on the part of doctors and nurses. More importantly, I can see all my own mistakes. I want to make a plea to bring about a change in the treatment of anorexia as found in too many hospitals in this country.

An eating disorder is a kind of defence from chaotic fears and feelings. It is not easy to overcome. The person with anorexia must acknowledge the illness—that is the first step to recovery, admitting a reality which has been denied before. After that there *might* be a possibility of change. Not wanting to accept help is *not* stubbornness. Anorexics who deny they are ill and are dragged off to see a doctor are not going to become motivated to get well.

Many a patient believes others see her as manipulative, cunning, deceitful, a liar. How many of us would not live up to these expectations, if we were made to feel we were all these things? Helping them to see that they are lovable and must learn to love themselves is very important.

Very gradually the patient has to learn to gain the control and security she requires in life from womanhood rather than from her illness. She must be re-taught how to eat; how to shop for food; how to cook food (without becoming frenetic); how to shop for clothes, how to develop relationships.

Weight targets should be very low—a patient weighing only 4½ stone, should be set a target weight of, say, 5 stone. When this is achieved and totally accepted by the patient, another should be set and so on until the patient is ready to accept a more normal weight.

Her family must be helped to look beyond guilt and blame and learn to cope. Anorexia must be explained clearly to them. They must be encouraged to examine what is happening within the family that might be perpetuating the problem. Many problems arise *after* the anorexia has been recognised. Most importantly, families should think of themselves as contributors to the anorexic's recovery rather than as the cause of the illness.

Encourage the person with anorexia to become part of a fellowship, a community, where they will be totally accepted for what they are. Once accepted they feel liked by others, then they can start to like themselves. That is the beginning of recovery.

I make this plea on behalf of those with anorexia that they may realise their worth beyond their looks and that they may learn to live life to the full without fear or panic.

What Is Anorexia

'A precise definition of anorexia nervosa is difficult because of the complexity and diversity of each individual case—the cause is deep rooted in the psyche of the individual and her relationship with her family and her environment, but in general terms it can be described as a syndrome which manifests itself as *loss of body weight, loss of body shape* and *cessation of menstruation*. This triad is the result of reduced food intake and failure to make the transition from puberty to womanhood.'

Dr Simon Dunbar,
Catherine's brother
From *Catherine* p. 131

Symptoms of anorexia often develop at times of unrest or change, and the pursuit of thinness is a frantic effort to establish a sense of control and identity. It is not a 'slimmers' disease.

Anorexia is a medical term for loss of appetite, but is more likely to be suppressed or denied appetite. Anorexic people are not so much repelled by food, as fascinated by it. Whether they begin by feeling they are the wrong size or merely use that feeling as an excuse to justify their peculiar eating habits, has not been established.

One in every hundred girls in their late teens is liable to suffer from anorexia. Girls are ten times more likely than boys to develop anorexia. One in every twenty sufferers dies from the illness. The typical first time victim is a girl aged 14–17 years.

Clinical Psychologist Peter Slade identifies two characteristics of anorexics:

1 Perfectionism—which creates dissatisfaction with every aspect of life.

2 A feeling of not being in control—that all you can control is yourself and, in particular, your body. Dieting is an easy form of control. It becomes addictive; a bit of a high, a way of coping with life.

The feeling of lack of control may be related to an introverted personality with low self esteem. Male anorexics are, in general, unassertive and inhibited. Anorexics often find it hard to express their feelings, feel isolated, and are obsessive. They have problems adjusting to puberty and feel pressured by future career decisions.

Anorexia is not confined to teenagers. Women in later life may develop it after a physical trauma such as miscarriage, physical illness or hysterectomy. Alcoholism can be triggered by anorexia in older women. In one alcoholic treatment unit it was found that over one-third of women admitted under the age of 40 had a history of anorexia before they ran into problems with alcohol.

The warning signs include withdrawing from other people such as school-friends; depression; intense competitiveness, including rivalry at home and at school; and obsessive working or exercising. Other people are encouraged to eat; and there is an increased interest in what others eat, in cooking and in food. Daily weighing, calorie counting and pre-occupation with body shape are common. Anxiety and panic attacks can occur, and there may be overactivity and increased mental alertness.

Distinguishing anorexia from normal teenage behaviour is not easy. Adolescents like privacy, are moody, feel anxious and even like to keep fit. Anorexics conceal their illness. Secrecy is all part of the need to maintain control. It is a question of degree, it is the extent of the change that is important. Jason, age 19, tells us: 'it's an escape that goes drastically wrong. You are cut off from all your feelings. And it's an incredibly selfish illness.

You're thinking about yourself the whole time. I spent my whole time thinking about food—thinking about it, but rejecting it'.

An anorexic's starved body reacts by closing down all non-essential activity. Circulation slows down and anorexics are almost always cold. To counter this, fine hair is produced all over the body, including the face. Even sitting down becomes painful because there is so little flesh on the bones. Other symptoms include kidney damage, loss of teeth and hair. When the weight drops to a life threatening level the body starts to feed on itself, and consumes its muscle.

Anorexia is difficult to treat because it is so complex. Most treatments focus on the problems of food intake. Renee Kauffer of *Anorexic Aid* tells sufferers:

'Treat food as a medicine. If your doctor prescribed medicine and told you to take it three times a day you would take it, even if it was nasty. What I am saying to you is—take your medicine. I'm not saying you will like it. Just take it.'

The very nature of the illness means that treatment frequently becomes a battle for control between the anorexic determined to keep what control she has and the doctors. The most successful treatment to date has been in counselling patients at a stage before the anorexia has become a total obsession.

Dos And Don'ts For Well-meaning Friends And Relatives

After 10 years of infertility, and 4 adopted children, Elsie Sieben and her husband conceived Jonathan who, tragically, lived only 18 hours. Two miscarriages occurred but then, 4 years later David was born. Unbelievably, he died at 5 months.

Elsie writes: four pregnancies, and no babies—the feelings of sadness, loss and failure are intense. Remembering how ignorant I was before this happened to us and knowing that invariably people are just trying to be helpful when they say things that would be better left unsaid, I offer this not as criticism but to help others understand and be supportive of those who suffer this grief:

• Don't ignore me because you are uncomfortable with the subject of death. It makes me wonder if what happened to me means nothing to you.

• Acknowledge my pain, even if you think I shouldn't be feeling it because I've lost 'only a baby'. And please don't expect me to be 'over this' in a month (or even a year or two); the depth of my grief will even shock me as it returns in waves over and over again, long after everyone else has forgotten. Holidays and the anniversaries of his birth and his death will be particularly difficult.

• If you haven't yet called and a long time has gone by, tell me that you are sorry that you just haven't known what to say, but *don't* say you've been too busy! This has been an extremely large event in my life and it hurts to hear it has been so low on your priority list that you couldn't spare a 5 or 10 minute call.

• If you invite me for lunch in the midst of my grief, expect me to talk about my loss. It's all I am thinking about anyway and I need to talk it out; small talk neither interests nor helps me now.

• Don't change the subject if I should start crying. Tears (and talking about it) are the healthiest way for me to release this intense emotion.

• Telling me that so-and-so's situation must have been harder to bear won't make mine easier. It only makes me feel you don't understand or can't acknowledge the extent of my pain.

• Don't expect that because 'he is in the presence of the Lord' that is all that should matter—that I should not be hurting. I do believe he is, and I'm thankful for that but my arms ache to hold him and I miss him so.

• Now is not the time to tell me all about your own birth experiences—it reminds me painfully that you came home with a live baby and I didn't.

• Telling me that I must be a very special person that God would send me such a heavy burden and 'God's will is best', implies that God purposely did this. I believe His will is best, too, but I don't believe everything that happens—including my baby's death or anyone being killed by a drunk driver, for instance—is God's will.

• Don't remind me that I'm so lucky to have the other kids. I am, I know it, but my pain is excruciating for *this* child and the others don't take that away.

• No matter how bad I look, please don't say 'You look terrible'. I feel like a total failure right now and I don't need to hear that I look awful too.

• Don't say 'I'm so glad you didn't get to hold him or nurse him'. I am in agony because I didn't get to do those things. My arms ache to hold him and my breasts are full of milk meant for him and the feeling of deprivation and missing my baby are so intense I can't imagine you'd believe it is easier for me this way.

• Don't devalue my baby. 'Oh well, better luck next time', etc.—to me he was a very special unique person and there is no way he can ever be replaced. Besides you don't know if there ever will be a next time—I don't either and that is a pain all its own.

• Don't say 'I know how you feel, I lost my mother. . .'. It is not the same. We all expect our parents to die one day after they have lived their lives, but I am intensely grieving for all the might-have-beens of my baby's life.

• When you ask my husband how I am doing don't forget to ask him how he's doing too. He also lost a son he was eagerly awaiting and if you ignore his hurt it says to him that his pain shouldn't exist or doesn't matter.

• Don't say 'You'd try again?' like I must be crazy. If you had my history you might not want to face menopause, without doing everything you could to change it, either.

• If I snap at you for saying any of the above—or anything else—please forgive me and try to understand it came from my intense pain. Your dog might bite you when you try to pick him up after he's been hit by a car—that wouldn't mean he hates you or is ungrateful, just that he's been hurt and your touch, well-intentioned though it be, has added more pain.

• Hug me, tell me that you care and that you're sorry this has happened.

• Be available to me often if you can and let me talk and cry without judging me. Saying 'don't be angry' is like saying 'don't be thirsty'. My feelings are part of a normal grief response and I will work through them quicker and easier if you aren't judgemental.

• Just love me and I will always remember you as a true friend.

The Compassionate Friends

Jillian Tallon, National Secretary
Compassionate Friends

The aim of *Compassionate Friends* is to provide understanding, comfort and support to bereaved parents whose lives have been shattered by the death, from whatever causes, of their child and sometimes children.

It is not possible to say 'this mode of death is worse than that'. To each parent, the death of their child (whether their only child, or one of several) is 100% tragedy and the shock and bewilderment are devastating.

Compassionate Friends provides the one thing that no-one else can. People who can say, 'I know'. Not 'I imagine', not 'I think', not 'I guess'—but 'I *know*'. I know the havoc into which your life has fallen, I know the agony that is ripping through your heart, the pain in your whole being. I know the bewilderment and the endless questioning of 'why' and 'if only'. But I know too, because I have been there, that 'recovery' is possible and will come in time and with help. You will never be the same person again, your values are forever changed, your needs and your perceptions too, but in time you will be able to live a 'normal' life again.

It is for these two purposes—'I know' and 'recovery will come in time'—that we exist.

Compassionate Friends is a befriending not a counselling organisation. The specific value of *Compassionate Friends* is the shared experience. In counselling organisations it is not a prerequisite that a counsellor be able to say to a client, 'I know from my own experience'. It is that which makes *Compassionate Friends* so different—and so needed.

The first contact will usually be with the Bristol Office. The telephone is answered by a bereaved parent, and the first thing they will do is *listen*. Relevant names and addresses can be offered later. Professionals who telephone on behalf of bereaved parents can be sent a leaflet with names and addresses of local contacts, as can friends and relatives. Sometimes grieving grandparents can be put in touch with each other. Links can be made, where requested, between parents whose children have died in similar circumstances.

At a local level, county secretaries are always available on the end of the telephone. They also organise meetings at their homes or even in pubs to bring together bereaved parents; particularly to introduce the newly bereaved to other parents.

Within *Compassionate Friends* there are two special groups, whose needs are those of any bereaved parents, but with the addition of a particular dimension; they are *Parents of Murdered Children* and the *Shadow of Suicide* groups. These groups offer the support of experience of the law and the media in particular, and the problems encountered with each of these.

For many people, the quarterly Newsletter is their lifeline. Made up mostly of contributions from parents, it ranges from the newly bereaved writing in raw agony and often anger to those further along the way, offering thoughts and suggestions of things they have found helpful. Also there are letters, appeals for contact, and topics of especial importance to bereaved parents.

There is also a variety of booklets and leaflets to help both the bereaved and those who meet them. The postal library can be another lifeline. A lot of bereaved people have a burning need to read as much as they can about the subject and draw much comfort and strength from this source.

The *Compassionate Friends*, though born through a clergyman's realisation of how much comfort two sets of bereaved parents drew from each other, is not a religious organisation; there are members of various faiths, and of none. Our only common bond is the loss of our child. There is no membership fee, we have all paid the highest price possible to become members of a group we never wanted to join. There is a subscription to the Newsletter, to cover the production costs, but this is waived wherever necessary.

In our Bristol office the telephone is answered by Anne Pocock, who is herself a bereaved mother. The line is open 9.30 am – 5 pm, Monday to Friday. Outside these hours there is an answering machine, which also gives a telephone number for parents who feel they must talk to someone immediately. The address and telephone number are given on p.79.

Appendix One

Further Reading

Books

After Suicide, John H Hewett
Westminster Press, Philadelphia (1980)

A Grief Observed, C S Lewis
Faber (1966)

The Anatomy of Bereavement: A Handbook for the Caring Professions, Beverley Raphael
Hutchinson (1984)

Anorexia Nervosa: A Guide for Sufferers and their Families, R L Palmer
Pelican (1980)

Anorexia Nervosa: Let Me Be, A H Crisp
Academic Press (1980)

The Art of Starvation: One Girl's Journey through Adolescence and Anorexia—A Story of Survival, Sheila MacLeod
Virago (1981)

Bereavement: Studies of Grief in Adult Life, Colin Murray Parkes
Tavistock Publications (1972)

Beyond Endurance: When A Child Dies, Ronald J Knapp
Schocken Books, New York (1986)

Birds of the Air, Alice Thomas Ellis
Duckworth (1980)

Care of the Child Facing Death, edited by Dr Lindy Burton
Routledge & Kegan Paul (1974)

*Catherine: The Story of a Young Girl who Died of Anorexia
Nervosa*, Maureen Dunbar
Viking (1986)

Children First and Always: A Portrait of Great Ormond Street,
Derrik and Gillian Mercer
Macdonald (1986)

The Chronically Ill Child: A Guide for Parents and Professionals,
Audrey T McCollum
New Haven & London Yale University Press (1975)

The Courage to Grieve, Judy Tatelbaum
Heineman (1981)

*The Damocles Syndrome: Psychosocial Consequences of Surviving
Childhood Cancer*, Gerald P Koocher and John E O'Malley
McGraw-Hill Book Co. (1981)

Death and the Family, Lily Pincus
Saber (1981)

*Don't Take My Grief Away from Me: What to Do When you Lose
a Loved One*, Doug Manning
Harper and Row (1985)

The Dying Child, Jo-Eileen Gyulay
McGraw–Hill Book Co. A Blakiston Publication (1978)

Facing Death: Patients, Families and Professionals,
Averil Stedeford
William Heinemann Medical Books Ltd (1984)

The Golden Cage (A picture of Anorexia), Hilde Bruch
Harvard University Press. Open Books (1977)

Help for the Bereaved, Kathleen Smith
Duckworth (1978)

The Last Song, Neil Gadsby
Poems written after the death of his daughter, Katherine, who
died of cancer.
Available from Rectory Gardens, Balscote, Banbury, Oxon.
Proceeds to Katherine House Hospice.

Letters Home, Letters of Sylvia Plath, edited by
Aurelia Schober Plath
Faber and Faber (1974)

*More Than Sympathy: The Everyday Needs of Sick and
Handicapped Children and their Families*, Richard Lansdown
Tavistock Publications (1980)

Motherhood and Mourning, L G Peppers and R J Knapp
Praeger, NY, (1980)

*The Negative Scream: A Story of Young People Who Took
an Overdose*, Sally O'Brien
Routledge & Kegan Paul (1985)

On Children and Death, Elisabeth Kübler-Ross
Macmillan (1983)

The Private Worlds of Dying Children, Myra Blueband-Langner
Princeton (1978)

The Savage God, A Alvarez
Weidenfeld (1971) Penguin (1974)

Suicide and Attempted Suicide Among Children and Adolescents,
Keith Hawton
Sage Publications (1986)

When Going to Pieces Holds You Together, William A Miller
Augsburg Publishing House, Minneapolis (1976)

Dear Stephen. . . , Anne Downey
Arthur Jones Ltd (1987)

Articles

A Son is Killed, Martin Colebrook
British Medical Journal Vol 287 (24.12.83)

Anorexia Nervosa: A Disease of Our Time (the need to make provision for it), Professor A H Crisp
Health & Hygiene Vol 2, No. 3. (1979)

Camilla's Own Story: A Psychiatric Social Worker's Account of a 13 Year Old Girl's Attempted Suicide, Roland Barnes
Community Care (19.6.86)

Mourning the Loss of a Newborn Baby: An article on the need for parents to be able to mourn the death of a stillborn child or a child who has died within the first few days of life,

Dr Gillain C Forrest
Bereavement Care Vol 2, No. 1. (1983)

Murder—The Aftermath: An article on parents of murdered children
Time Out Jan 14-21 (1987)

Out of the Lives of Babes: An article on the struggle a family had to go through in dealing with the unresolved grief of the loss of a son

Community Care (17.7.86)
Reflections on Death in Childhood, Frances Dominica

British Medical Journal Vol 294, (10.1.87)

When A Child Dies, Jane Kerr Wood—describes issues faced when setting up a group for bereaved parents
Community Care (8.5.86)

Appendix Two

Counselling and Bereavement Organisations

General Groups

Association of Carers
First Floor
21–23 New Road
Chartham
Kent
ME4 4JQ
Tel. 0634 813981

Objects: To offer advice, support and opportunities for self-help carers of the disabled and/or elderly.
Activities: Self-help groups meet nationwide; information services.
Publications: Newsletters (bi-monthly) *Who Cares*, *Help at Hand: a Signpost Guide for Carers*.

Bereaved Parents Helpline
6 Canons Gate
Harlow
Essex

Tel. 0279 412745

Contact: Charlotte
Parents who have lost children offer support by telephone and make visits locally.

Compassionate Friends
6 Denmark Street
Bristol
BS1 5DQ
Tel: 0272 292778

Contact: Anne Pocock
Objects: To offer friendship to grieving parents who have lost a child of any age through illness, accident, murder or suicide.
Activities: Support and friendship are offered to newly-bereaved families by bereaved parents who are representatives of Compassionate Friends. Local groups are run throughout the country.

CRUSE
National Organisation for the Widowed and their Children
Cruse House
126 Sheen Road
Richmond
Surrey
TW9 1UR
Tel: 01 940 4818/9407

Contact: Barbara Pentreach
Objects: To offer a service of counselling and opportunities for social contact to people who have lost a relative.
Activities: Training courses for professional and lay people involved with the dying and bereaved. Over 100 branches. A wide range of supportive literature.

Publications: Begin Again, Helping the Widowed, Cruse Chronicle (all monthly); *Bereavement Care* (quarterly).

Family Welfare Association
296 Wellingborough Road
Northampton
NN1 4EP
Tel: 0604 20341

21 Kempson Road
London SW6
Tel. 01 736 2127

Contact: Mrs Eileen Fox (Northampton)
Offers counselling to people who are bereaved and encourages the setting up of self-help groups.

Contact: Mr Robert Tollemache (London)
Offers counselling to people who are bereaved.

Foundation For Black Bereaved Families
11 Kingston Square
Salters Hill
London SE19
Tel. 01 761 7228

Organiser: Lorreene Hunte

Jewish Bereavement Counselling Service
1 Cyprus Gardens
London N3 1SP
Tel. 01 349 0839 or 01 387 4300 ext. 227

Samaritans Incorporated
17 Uxbridge Road
Slough
Berks
SL1 1SN
Tel. 0753 32713

Contact: Louise Ensoll
Objects: To help the suicidal and despairing.
Activities: There are 180 Samaritan local branches in the UK and Irish Republic. The Samaritans offer a 24-hour widely publicised absolutely confidential service for people who are in despair, or feel suicidal.

Specific

Anorexic Aid
The Priory Centre
11 Priory Road
High Wycombe
Bucks HP13 6SL

Contact: Renee Kauffer, 17 Brittain Close, Elstree, Herts.
Objects and Activities: To offer support and mutual self-care to those suffering from or concerned with anorexia and bulimia nervosa, and to promote education and understanding about the illness, through a network of self-help groups.
Publications: Magazine (quarterly).

Anorexics Anonymous
Tel. 01 748 3994

Advice and counselling about anorexia and other compulsive eating disorders.

Anorexic Family Aid And National Information Centre
Sackville Place
44/48 Magdalen Street
Norwich
Norfolk
NR3 1JE
Tel. 0603 621414

Chairman: Nancy Pearce
Objects: To offer help, support and understanding to anyone suffering from anorexia or bulimia nervosa, and their families and friends. To collect and disseminate information at a local and nation level.
Activities: Local group meetings; the National Information Centre offers personal contact by telephone and post; regular newsletters; book reviews; action guidelines; educational material; nationwide information;
Publications: Feedback (newsletter). List available.

BACUP
British Association for Cancer United Patients, Families and Friends
121–123 Charterhouse Street
London EC1
Tel. 01 608 1661

Offers information, advice and emotional support to cancer patients, and their families and friends by telephone and post. Five lines open Mon – Fri 09.30 – 17.00. Until 19.00 Tues and Thurs.
Publications: Newsletter three times yearly as well as specialist leaflets.

Cancer Link
46a Pentonville Road
London N1 9HE
Tel. 01 833 2451

Contact: Amanda Kelsey
Objects: To provide information about cancer and the forms of emotional and practical support available to people with cancer, their relatives and friends. To promote the formation of support groups, with training and back-up.
Activities: Support Groups hold open meetings, often with a speaker, and smaller meetings, where people can share their experiences. Volunteers who are trained by Cancer Link give phone advice or visit homes or hospitals. An information service is based at the above address.

The CLIC Trust
The Cancer and Leukaemia in Childhood Trust
CLIC House
12 Fremantle Square
Cotham
Bristol BS6 5TL
Tel. 0272 426217

Offers support to children with leukaemia and their families. The support is given in a variety of ways, the most important being accommodation at CLIC House in Bristol which caters for up to 40 people at a time.

The Emma Killingback Memorial Fund
57 Blackbush Avenue
Chadwell Heath
Romford
Essex RM6 5TT
Tel. 01 599 5643

John and Carole Killingback started a memorial fund when their daughter Emma died of neuroblastoma. They are raising money for research into the disease. John and Carole are also happy to offer 'a listening ear' to parents whose children have died of this illness.

Family Welfare Association
Hill Farm House
Old Groveway
Simpson
Milton Keynes
MK6 3AA
Tel. 0908 678237/8

Contact: Anne Codd
A specialist counselling service to people who feel suicidal or
have already attempted suicide.

Foundation For Study Of Infant Deaths
(Cot Death Research and Support)
15 Belgrave Square
London SW1X 8PS
Tel. 01 235 0965

Objects: To promote and sponsor research into the causes and
prevention of sudden and unexpected deaths (cot deaths/sudden
infant death syndrome): to support and counsel bereaved parents; to be a centre for information and exchange of knowledge
in the UK and abroad.
Activities: Offers personal support and information to bereaved
families from the London office and local parent groups.
Sponsors research; publishes material on research findings and
counselling needs.
Publication: Newsletter (bi-annually). List available.

Gay Switchboard
Tel. 01-837 7324

24-hour information and help service for homosexual women
and men.

Kaleidoscope Youth and Community Project
40-46 Cromwell Road
Kingston on Thames
Surrey
Tel. 01 549 2681/7488

Contact: Eric Blakebrough
Community-based centre providing non-intensive counselling and recreational facilities for young people. Also Medical Surgery—Fri: 10 pm – 6 pm. (The centre includes a hostel (capacity 21) providing rehabilitation support for young people (16-22) for up to 12 months.) Hours: helpful to phone for opening hours of different facilities.

Leukaemia Care Society
PO Box 82
Exeter
Devon
EX2 5DP
Tel. 0392 218514

Objects: To promote the welfare of people suffering from leukaemia and that of their families, and also the welfare of those families who have lost relatives from the disease.
Activities: The Society provides information, support, financial help and holidays.
Publications: Newsletter.

London Youth Advisory Centre
26 Prince of Wales Road
Kentish Town
London NW5 3LG
Tel. 01 267 4792

Offers a counselling, advisory and information service to young

people and their parents.
Hours: Mon–Fri: 9.30 am – 5 pm plus evening appointments.

Miscarriage Association
18 Stonybrook Close
West Bretton
Wakefield
West Yorkshire WF4 4TP
Tel. 0924 85515

Objects: To provide information and support for women and
their families both during and after miscarriage.
Activities: To advance education on the emotional as well as
physical effects of miscarriage, with the help and advice of doctors and medical staff. Support groups have been organised
throughout the country.
Publications: Newsletter (quarterly, to members), leaflets,
posters.

National Association Of Victims Support Schemes
17a Electric Lane
Brixton
London
SW9 8JLA
Tel. 01 737 2010

Director: Helen Reeves OBE
Contact: John Ponting
Objects: To co-ordinate the work of local schemes designed to
meet the varied needs of victims of crime. A small Working
Party has been convened under the auspices of NAVSS to discuss
the lack of support for families of Homicide victims and ways in
which this could be improved.

Neuroblastoma Society
Janet and Neville Oldridge
Woodland
Ordsall
Park Road
Retford
Notts. DN22 7PJ
Tel. 0777 709238

This is a medical research charity raising funds for research into neuroblastoma and giving support to parents. They have a network of local representatives; usually parents who have had children with neuroblastoma. They can be telephoned at any time.
Publications Booklet to give help to parents in understanding the disease.

Parents Of Murdered Children Support Group
Compassionate Friends
10 Eastern Avenue
Southend-on-Sea
Essex SS2 5QU
Tel. 0702 68510

Organiser: Ann Robinson
Parents of murdered children have formed a group within Compassionate Friends. The idea is for members to help each other by listening compassionately, sharing feelings and experiences and being supportive particularly at traumatic times such as a trial.

Parents Lifeline
Station House
73d Stapleton Hall Road
London N4 3QF
Tel. 01 263 2265

Support for parents whose children are critically ill in hospital.

PROPS
Parents Recognition of Paediatric Errors
51, The Orchard
Newton
Swansea
SA3 4UQ
Tel. 0792 367550

Organiser: Joan Bye
Support organisation for parents who feel their child has died as a result of incorrect diagnosis and wrong treatment. Can help parents who are dissatisfied with their child's treatment seek further medical advice.

SOS (Survivors Of Suicide/Living In The Shadow Of Suicide)
Compassionate Friends
Blair Gowrie
13 Wood Road
Halewood
Liverpool 261 UY
Tel. 051 486 1236

Organiser: Audrey Walsh
This is a new group formed within the Compassionate Friends. Parents of children who have taken their own lives are put in touch with others who have experienced the same loss. Also aim to further research and education into prevention of suicide and questions arising from suicide.

Stillbirth And Neonatal Death Society (SANDS)
Argyle House
29–31 Euston Road
London NW1 2SD

Tel. 01 833 2851

Contact: Ms Lesley Moreland
Objects: To encourage research into the causes of neonatal death;
to establish a national network of parents willing to help others
similarly bereaved; to encourage awareness in professionals and
the public of the needs of parents and the long-term effects of
such deaths on the family.
Activities: Recruiting and training befrienders; organising local
groups; educating hospitals and the general public.
Publications: Notes on Initial Visit by a Befriending Parent etc.

Victims Helpline
St Leonards
Nuttall Street
London N1 5LZ ·
Tel. 01 729 1252

Co-ordinator: Jane Cobill
A 24-hour counselling service for anyone in distress as a result of
crime. They will try and arrange follow up support if requested.

Appendix Three

Dinah's Diary

Dinah Lawley started a diary after her son, Jamie, died in September 1985. The following are some extracts from that diary.

Two weeks later

How can you write a hole in your heart, a whole, a hole in your being. An ache, a loss, a thousand miles wide and deep, too deep to ever fill or close. I can't remember who I was before this happened. Each day is a challenge—each day and night contains a host of pitfalls, the abyss, the agony always at my side, like a companion clutching for life.

Three months later

I cannot hold my son again
I cannot touch his hair
I know he's gone for ever
I know I don't know where

I know I'm glad I had him
I know I loved him so

I know there's no returning
I know I must let go

I know my body's aching
I know with rage I shake
I cannot hold my son again
I know my heart will break

Five months later

Dear Jamie

I have all these photos, these drawings, these thoughts and these memories. Are they going to be enough? I am so glad you were/ are my son. I find it impossible to use the past tense about you: to make you a 'was'. I wish I could be sure that you knew I loved you, was proud of you (fervently), admired and respected you. I didn't have time to tell you all this. Your talent for life leaves me in the shade and I want to tell you that you are teaching me so much now. It is hard not to be able to talk to you, and see your grin, and know you will NEVER give me a hug again. Such simple things, so easily taken for granted, which mean more than the world to me now. Shock and disbelief still stun me as the fact of your death continues to work its way through me. All things you might have done, who you would have been—all that is stolen by this death. This death of yours/of ours, for you must know that we share it.

Thank you Jamie for your life with us and please keep on helping me to learn how to live.

I love you,

Dinah xx

Six months later

As I sit here in bed it's six months since you died, all but two days. Where are you now Jamie?

Your voice has been haunting me this morning, singing your old Beatle songs and I am greedy for those moments that were ours.

I remember the day you died and the night before. On the Friday evening I had worked at Willow, the new vegetarian restaurant, with Rosie and Isabel. We'd all been strung out one way or another—Rosie a period—myself a migraine and Isabel very tired.

I spoke to you late that night and said you really should get to sleep but you reminded me it was your special music programme. I said goodnight to you.

The next morning Brian Nicolson rang to let us know he'd worked out a way for you to go back to Foxhole. Excited we all stood in your room or sat on your bed, Peter, Laurel and I, as we talked about this wonderful turn of events. Laurel suggested you could stop doing your Kevicks homework now as it was no longer your school. The delight spread across your face as you fully realised the implications. I wanted you to know that you were going back, not because I'd pressurised people, but because they wanted you and thought a lot of you.

So then it was full speed to get up there (Foxhole) and break the news to friends. I managed to persuade you to eat at least a slice of toast, and then I'd give you a lift on my way to Totnes.

My head still hurt. It had hurt all week and I had cried and cried, worrying about you.

I last saw you where I dropped you.

We arrived at the turning for Foxhole and arranged for you to return by six. You wouldn't be having any lunch. Later I wondered if I'd given you money for lunch perhaps you wouldn't have been so light-headed. But we all looked for ways to blame ourselves—to take the guilt.

You turned and grinned, all tatters as usual, and that was it. I never saw you alive again; only completely dead at the mortuary and the bottom half of you lying dead or dying on the tarmac at Foxhole. People in uniforms covered the top half of you and I was kept away.

We waited for my mother and Geoff at High Cross. I waited for a couple of hours before I could gather myself to tell Laurel. Paddy eventually collected her from Ursula Crickmay's where she had gone after singing at a wedding at St. Mary's.

Laurel was brought to Jeannie and Paddy's bedroom and her reaction on being told was immediate and extreme. I wanted to hold her tight, to somehow protect her, but she fought to get loose and cried: 'It hurts—ow—ow—.'

The adults in the room seemed to be a little released by her reactions and the tears came down.

Somehow the time passed. Jo was there and Josie, and later when mum and Geoff arrived, we went to Bantham for what was the longest, darkest night and the worst twenty-four hours of my life.

The next day Laurel and I screamed into the sand for our boy, Laurel held by mum and Geoff, and me by Peter. I was a very old lady that day, could barely walk, could only feel in every cell pain and heartbreak.

I could not conceive of ever being able to live 'normally' again, not for one second.

My mother washed me in the bath. We thought of you, mostly at first lying in the pool of blood, but slowly the lifetimes memories returned and ever since I have been remembering.

You were so gentle, your hands especially had that beautiful reaching out quality that was also your father's—I'll always remember you reaching out towards something small and furry or someone young and vulnerable. Those hands carried no threat, no violence. You looked after me when I was ill, with those hands and it is sad that you were just becoming a man—the hands were large and strong yet so soft, so sensitive.

Later, when you were at Kevicks, a young teacher came up to Foxhole, so impressed was he with you that he wanted to see what kind of school had produced you.

You were kind to the kids in your music class at Kevicks, patiently helping those who had not your skill or talent. You had always been kind.

You were my mother's shining light, the boy she'd never had

and you were so close. I know she mourns as I do.

As my mind swells with the flood of memories, the sun shines and lights the grass. A bird hops along and I think of your grave alive with colour, flowers chaotically pushing up, even in the grass around. Just like you, bursting out, busy with energy. You vibrated with life and now you vibrate in death. But you were also so very vulnerable, wide-eyed and open, and I hurt you a lot. I see now your shock and pain when I vented my anger on you—you dumb with disbelief, me shaking with rage at your silence.

Oh my darling, forgive me please. This is such a hard lesson to bear.

Soon I'm going to take a photo of your grave. Now, at the six month mark, I want to show how life moves on, how we all move on without you. Yet you, your essence, your memory, have never been closer than now.

You travel everywhere with me, although sometimes I'm happier when you're a little distant and I can be a bit separate. Sometimes your closeness (but without a body) makes me cry and cry. Self-pity I suppose. But I wouldn't have you leave me.

God bless, my golden boy, God bless. With my breaking heart laughing I'll live, as we all must, with death over our left shoulder and life a golden, glorious moment, a gift, a vision, an illusion.

Who can say what the truth is?

Eighteen months later

In many ways I am 'better'. Yet it is not over, nor do I feel it ever will be because this death of his, of ours, has put me on a new path of self-discovery. I have been lucky. The things that helped me most were available in me. The Elisabeth Kübler-Ross, 'Life, Death and Transition' workshop enabled me to find an outlet for the anger, rage and grief which isn't really available in ordinary life. There is almost nowhere where it is acceptable to be *that* angry, to feel *that* much pain.

The aim of the LDT workshops is to enable people to express those huge feelings, so that you don't swallow them. If we repress these feelings they can be massively harmful to the whole being. Research has shown that the immune system can be severely affected by the stress of bereavement. Bottling it up increases this effect and England is probably the worst place in the world for putting on a 'brave face' and not acknowledging the depth of our feelings.

Bitterness, it seems to me, is a direct result of not being able to express the anger one feels at the colossal devastation of one's child being taken for ever.

Another thing that really helps is to be able to talk and talk until there is nothing left to say, even though you repeat yourself endlessly. The torment of remembering, feeling pain, going over and over the facts is all part of the healing and if all this is thoroughly experienced and not avoided, in the end it starts to fade away. One day I simply knew that Jamie was now in my heart for ever and that he could never be removed. Consciously I think of him much less, yet he is always with me, inside me and it doesn't hurt. In fact it's a good, warm feeling.

I have had to learn new ways of treating myself. I have to respond more sensitively to my inner needs, be more gentle with myself, push myself less. Life isn't what it was and in some ways it's infinitely worse, yet there are very positive signs. I am much more accepting about all kinds of things. I am learning to let go, trying not to push the mind so much.

Everything is touched by this kind of loss; health, the ability to work, relationships, all can suffer. Gradually as the time passes the hopeful aspects emerge, sometimes it's just a new enthusiasm for life, sometimes it's deeper compassion and understanding of other people, sometimes it's simply the development of humility in the face of this strange universe of ours.

After he died I knew I was in a dark valley, an alien territory where I feel there were no signposts telling me where to go. I was lost and hurting and alone. But even then I was helped. I instinctively knew that there was darkness and light and that, although for the time I had no choice but to be in the darkness, one day it would be light again. Knowing this I was able to read, write, draw and talk my through the wilderness. Mostly I seemed to need to be alone. Now it is light again, not the blinding mid-day sun but a gentle dawn. I still want to be perfectly healed right now, or preferably yesterday and I still have to continue to accept that it all takes a long time and that it cannot be rushed.

I am learning so much from this experience. It has given me new eyes to see with and a new heart to feel with. Once more the world is a beautiful place and I am so grateful for the time I did have with my son. I also feel much closer to my daughter and truly value her. We've been through a lot together and she has given me wonderful support. The experience has deepened her and given her understanding beyond her years.

There are still difficulties I have to face. The relationship I was in has broken up, I was unable to work for a long time, there are financial problems, and my health has been unreliable. I have faith though, that if I can emerge solidly from the darkness that was the result of my beautiful son's death, I can certainly cope with these problems.

What lies ahead I don't know. What I want to do is obtain the funding to return to university to study psychology and counselling in order to eventually work within the system and using my own experience of this tragedy to help others. As I already have an English degree, I have been unable to get a grant and yet I am sure that eventually a way will somehow be found.

One last thing, is that I have met other people who share the experience of losing a child. These relationships have been very special to me and continue to offer incredible love and support.